PRAISE FOR *A CLEAN HEART*

"Set in 1991 in the early days of chemical dependency treatment, John Rosengren's *A Clean Heart* follows the daily routine of Carter, a young counselor at a teen treatment facility. The book, which switches back and forth from Carter's troubled childhood to present day, provides a wealth of details and insight into the daily life and struggles of both staff and residents at a typical treatment center of the time. [This is] a novel that will strike a chord with readers wrestling with substance abuse, the Catholic faith, or family trauma."

—Alison McGhee, author of *Shadow Baby* and *Never Coming Back*

"With echoes of *One Flew Over the Cuckoo's Nest*, Rosengren writes with great empathy for the misfits and outsiders of Six West (whose halls are stalked by the unforgettable Sister X). *A Clean Heart* grapples with life's most difficult puzzles: how we navigate the tangled bonds of family and how we save ourselves, ultimately, by becoming vulnerable. A redemptive and affecting novel."

—Will McGrath, author of *Everything Lost Is Found Again*

"*A Clean Heart* picks at the knot of addiction and recovery insistently and with a wholesomeness intriguingly at odds with its subject. I enjoyed this book."

—Thomas Beller, author of *The Sleep-Over Artist*

"In his powerful new book, *A Clean Heart*, John Rosengren reminds us that the journey of body and soul is best taken with another, or others, that somehow tie their healing to our own. Set in a rehab center for teens, each level of recovery—or descent—is housed in a character. Whether client or employee, they are recognizable, flawed, [and] at times hilarious and lovable in their struggles. This is a book of lessons and offered insights, but never at the expense of a well-told and gripping story."

—Kevin Kling, author of *The Dog Says How* and *Holiday Inn*

"In *A Clean Heart*, John Rosengren has created a wonderfully empathetic protagonist in Carter and a wonderfully complicated situation. After seven years in A.A., Carter finds himself being tested both by a new patient at the rehabilitation unit where he works and by his boss, the charismatic Sister Xavier. The result is a gripping and suspenseful novel about the dangerous art of helping."

—Margot Livesey, author of *The Flight of Gemma Hardy*

PRAISE FOR *A CLEAN HEART*

"Set in 1991 in the early days of chemical dependency treatment, John Rosengren's *A Clean Heart* follows the daily routine of Carter, a young counselor at a teen treatment facility. The book, which switches back and forth from Carter's troubled childhood to present day, provides a wealth of details and insight into the daily life and struggles of both staff and residents at a typical treatment center of the time. [This is] a novel that will strike a chord with readers wrestling with substance abuse, the Catholic faith, or family trauma."

— Alison McGhee, author of *Shadow Baby* and *Never Coming Back*

"With echoes of *One Flew Over the Cuckoo's Nest*, Rosengren writes with great empathy for the misfits and outsiders of Six West (whose halls are stalked by the unforgettable Sister X). *A Clean Heart* grapples with life's most difficult puzzles: how we navigate the tangled bonds of family and how we save ourselves, ultimately, by becoming vulnerable. A redemptive and affecting novel."

— Will McGrath, author of *Everything Lost Is Found Again*

"Rosengren's *A Clean Heart* thrums with vibrant characters yearning to do the right thing, often at great personal costs to themselves. Witty and totally absorbing, here is a novel about helping those snared by drugs and alcohol see that they, too, are worthy of love. Along the way, the characters learn that painful memories and secrets are a type of drug in their own right— that the past is just as mind-altering and addictive as anything found in a syringe or shot glass. Both heartbreaking and heart-lifting, this is a narrative about coming clean that will haunt the imagination long after the last page has been read. Spellbinding, mesmerizing, and deeply human, this is fiction about the toxins and tonics that beat in all of our hearts."

—Patrick Hicks, author of *The Commandant of Lubizec* and *Library of the Mind*

A
CLEAN
HEART

A
CLEAN
HEART

a novel

JOHN ROSENGREN

mango
PUBLISHING

CORAL GABLES

Cover Design, Layout & Design: Morgane Leoni

Author Photo: © Scott Streble

For permission requests, please contact the publisher at:

Mango Publishing Group

2850 S Douglas Road, 2nd Floor

Coral Gables, FL 33134 USA

info@mango.bz

For special orders, quantity sales, course adoptions and corporate sales, please email the publisher at sales@mango.bz. For trade and wholesale sales, please contact Ingram Publisher Services at customer.service@ingramcontent.com or +1.800.509.4887.

A Clean Heart: A Novel

Library of Congress Cataloging-in-Publication number: 2020933492

ISBN: (print) 978-1-64250-192-6, (ebook) 978-1-64250-193-3

BISAC category code FIC043000, FICTION / Coming of Age

Printed in the United States of America

To Pat Meyer, Jerry Stelli, Ralph Bruce, Rich Scanlon, Pat Bixler, and Audrey at Parkview West. Thanks for showing me the way.

Something we were withholding made us weak
until we found out that it was ourselves
we were withholding from our land of living
and forthwith found salvation in surrender.

−Robert Frost

CHAPTER 1

Oscar sauntered down the hall, hips stiff, shoulders swaggering, hands cuffed behind his back. Contempt crusted his face. He looked neither left nor right at the calligraphy slogans framed on the walls: "First Things First," "Live and Let Live," "Easy Does It." His eyes bored straight ahead, cleared his path. The other kids watched from their bedroom doorways in quiet awe, reverence almost. They shrank back when he passed. Even with his hands cuffed and a cop at his elbow, Oscar sauntered down the hallway with savage independence. His eyes fixed on the counselor waiting for him: *Fuck you.*

Carter knew the look. The defiance, the determination. His mother, after a few drinks.

Once inside the counselor's office, Oscar's granite-gray eyes alone sliced the silence. He would not speak. The tough ones usually didn't. His glare dared Carter to try to make him.

Oscar embodied defiance. More than the dirty brown hair shaken over his shoulders, more than the faded jean jacket with the Guns 'N Roses patch emblazoned across the back, more than the torn black jeans—the spirit of his defiance was greater than the sum of these singular details. He looked like many of the kids who had sat in Carter's office, but a violence smoldered in him that made the other kids seem like Gandhi in their noncooperation.

Officer Patterson packed the handcuffs back into his belt. "I'll wait outside."

"Thanks, Charlie." Carter regarded Oscar. "I don't think that'll be necessary."

Patterson shrugged. Carter noted the slight shake of his head on the way out and knew he was muttering to himself. Patterson was old school. He saw only the ones who didn't make it.

Oscar's glare followed the cop out the door.

Carter faced Oscar, now seated on the chrome-frame chair, the handcuffs gone, his hands poised unseen in his jean pockets. Carter was sure they were packed in fists. When he addressed Oscar, the punk clenched his jaw.

"So, Rock Lake or this place, and you chose the lesser of two evils. Why?"

Oscar fixed him with a look of scorn. *What do you think, dumbfuck?*

Carter continued as though he had answered politely. "If you finish treatment, the judge might suspend your sentence.

But you've got to finish treatment. We're under no orders to keep you. It's up to you whether you stay."

Oscar snorted. His street clothes clashed with the hospital decor. He belonged to the street—roaming alleys, preying upon car stereos, staking his territory with spray paint—instead of being boxed within the lime-green walls of Carter's office.

"Another thing," Carter said. "There are no bars, no locks here. You can walk anytime. If you stay, it's because you want to."

Oscar nodded sarcastically in agreement. He wasn't buying the tough guy, this-is-the-way-it-is approach.

"If you decide to stay, we're here to help."

The gentle tone achieved no better effect. Oscar scoffed at Carter, taking in his slender build, blond curls, and thin nose. *Wimp.*

Oscar's eyes paced the room, surveyed its contents. The olive-drab metal file cabinet, a pedestal for the yellowed Mr. Coffee; the particleboard desk with the faux mahogany veneer; the ficus in the corner; the hanging ferns; the orange, closely cropped carpet—"a shag with a crew cut," Carter joked. Oscar's eyes did not break stride. The North Stars pennant, the *Far Side* 1991 calendar (still on February; Carter had not yet flipped it to March), the cluttered desk.

"When I was seventeen, I sat in your chair and wanted out," Carter said. "You know what made me stay?"

Oscar gazed out the window. The university campus lay across the river, a shadow through the falling snow.

"I thought if I stayed long enough, they would teach me how to smoke pot without getting caught."

Oscar stared at the snowflakes swallowed by the icy black water six floors below.

"Instead, they taught me I didn't have to be a slave to drugs," Carter continued. "I've been sober since. Seven years."

Oscar turned to him. *Is this bullshit over yet?*

Self-disclosure wasn't going to work, Carter realized. They were too different. On the surface at least. He sensed they were the same deep down. He could sniff the addict in this kid.

The two sat for a moment locked in a silent showdown, Oscar smoldering, Carter pensive. He searched for a hidden door through Oscar's defiance.

"You hungry?"

He didn't flinch.

Carter buzzed the nurses' station. "Judy, I need a favor. Would you please bring me a sandwich, uh, roast beef and Swiss—" Carter raised his eyebrows at Oscar, who shrugged his shoulders almost imperceptibly. "And a pop."

"Carter, is this your idea of a joke?"

"For the new admit."

"Mustard or mayonnaise?"

Carter looked to Oscar.

"Mustard," he muttered.

"And an extra slice of cheese," Carter added.

"Coming right up."

Carter wasn't fooled. He knew Judy was still pissed that Sister Mary Xavier had asked Carter specifically to handle Oscar's admission. Judy had already laid out all of the forms on the countertop waiting for Oscar's arrival when he told her.

"We don't ask to do your work," she had said. "Stay away from ours."

"Sister X asked me to do it. I didn't volunteer. Believe me, I've got enough work of my own."

"Is that why you don't do your charting?"

"I'm behind because I get asked to do extra work."

"So stick to your own work if you can't finish it. Patient admissions are a nurse's responsibility."

"Come on. How hard can it be? Ask a few questions from a form."

That had been the wrong thing to say.

"Fine. Do it. Have it your way. But if you don't get it right, don't expect me to fix it for you. After all, it's only *a few questions from a form*."

"Judy, what I meant was—"

She shoved the forms at him. "I'll stay out of your way. Live and let live."

Thinking of Judy slapping mustard onto a slice of bread

and chastising him under her breath, Carter wondered if he would have been better off making Oscar's sandwich himself. He shuffled through the clutter of papers on his desk without finding what he wanted. Finally, his hand landed on a purple folder. He handed it to Oscar. "Inside you will find the scout rules and campfire songs. Memorize your cabin cheer."

Oscar didn't smile, and he didn't take the offered folder.

Carter knew his jokes wouldn't earn him a living, but he thought they might loosen up this kid. Instead, Oscar sat before him amused as stone.

"Seriously, read this. It'll tell you all about Six West: the daily schedule, the level system, consequences, privileges, et cetera."

Oscar scowled at the folder.

"Don't think of it as submission to someone else's rules. Think of it more as a willingness to try someone else's way that might work better than yours has—or hasn't."

The fight came back into his eyes.

"Give it a chance."

Oscar contemplated the folder, finally snatched it, and placed it under his thigh.

The knock on the door startled them both. Judy smiled past Carter with a plastic tray in her hands: the sandwich on a plate, neatly sliced into quarters, decorated with potato chips and a pickle, accompanied by a glass of Sprite with ice and a straw. As a bonus, she had added a pudding snack. "Room service."

"Thanks, Judy. Meet Oscar." Then, to him, "Judy is the head nurse on Six West."

Judy handed Oscar the tray. "Welcome."

He balanced the tray across his thighs and stuffed a full quarter of the sandwich into his mouth.

"Whoa. Judy dropped everything to make that for you. I want you to thank her, or I'll have her take it away."

"Oh, Carter, don't be silly. The poor boy's just hungry."

"Judy, please. Oscar?"

"Thanks," Oscar mumbled without looking up.

"Don't mention it," Judy chimed on her way out.

Carter resolved not to let her interfere with Oscar. The new admit gobbled chips while he chewed the last bite of his sandwich. Carter wondered if he had the munchies. Other kids had come over from Juvenile stoned, but Oscar didn't have that distracted air. Carter figured he probably was simply reacting to real food after a week of jail slop. He had yet to meet a teenage boy who wasn't perpetually hungry. The urine test would show whether Carter's hunch was correct.

"So, what's it going to be?"

Oscar dug into the pudding with the spoon. Carter noticed the stump below the knuckle of his right middle finger. It looked more like a scar than a birth defect.

"Well?"

Oscar raised his eyes slowly, pained. "What's what going to be, dude?

"You going to stay or not?"

Oscar slammed the pudding down on the tray. "You ruin my fucking appetite."

"Does that mean you won't be staying?"

A tense moment passed before he finally shrugged.

"What's that mean?"

"What the fuck you think it means?"

Stay calm, Carter told himself. *Just another angry kid.* "Not sure. I don't read shoulders."

"Then read my lips, fuckhead. I'll stay."

Carter couldn't help grinning to himself. *Guess I walked into that one. But at least he committed.* "Carter."

"What?"

"Carter. That's my name. Carter Kirchner. See, up on the wall." He pointed to the Chemical Dependency Practitioner certificate in the cheap, black metal frame hanging on the wall. Oscar's eyes didn't budge. "That's what you call me. Try it."

"Carter. Carter Kirchner," he said in a mocking tone. Then added under his breath, "Faggot."

Carter let it pass. "You'll get used to it. Let's get down to business." He pulled out one of the forms Judy had given him. He hated these forms, the endless piles of mundane paperwork, but sometimes they served as useful props, giving him an excuse to pry. "I need to get some background information. Full name?"

"Peter F. Pan."

Carter looked up. Oscar glared back.

"How do you spell your last name, Oscar?"

He spoke in the tone that adults use with small children, "D. U. R. A. N."

That's the way they got through much of the rest of the biographical data: Mother's maiden name? "Eve." The last time you saw your father? "The day he left home." Which was? "The last time I saw him." Oscar begrudgingly provided the most basic information. Until Carter asked, "How did you get arrested?"

A wave of sadness flickered in his eyes. He quickly averted them, but not before Carter glimpsed it.

Oscar pulled a pack of Marlboros from his jean jacket pocket, slid out a cigarette, tamped it against the meaty part of his palm, then clenched it between his lips. He didn't take his flat eyes off Carter. He slipped a pack of matches from his pocket, pried one match loose, and closed the book, slowly turning it in his hand.

"You can't smoke in my office."

Oscar spread his hands apart in surprise. "I *can't*?" He set the match against the book to strike it. "Watch me."

Carter hated this part, having to be the enforcer. "Part of the program. One of the rules. Without them, it wouldn't work. We've all got to live by them."

He struck the match and raised it to his cigarette. "And if I don't?"

"You forfeit smoking privileges for a full day, twenty-four hours."

He shrugged his eyebrows, amused, and moved the lit match toward the tip of his cigarette.

Carter snapped. "Don't you understand? You're here on a prayer. This is your last chance. You fuck up here, that's it, you're in jail, ten months minimum. You think you don't like me telling you not to smoke, believe me, it's a lot better than some fat fuck bending you over a toilet."

Carter paused to catch his breath. "Give yourself a chance."

Oscar glowered at him. Carter met his eyes evenly. The lit match still beside his cigarette, Oscar let it burn down to the stump of his middle finger. He did not flinch when the flame extinguished against his flesh. Slowly he spread his fingers and let the match drop to the floor. He kept the unlit cigarette clamped between his lips.

"So, tell me how you got arrested."

"Ask Officer Handcuffs."

"I'm asking you."

Oscar began the story of the night a week earlier. It was

late, past midnight, when he found his way back to the mission downtown. The doors were locked, so he went halfway round the block to a doorway in the alley. He had slept there before when he'd shown up too late at the mission. Often. Others knew it as his place. Called it "Oscar's crib." But that night he found an old man crouched in the doorway, asleep. Oscar nudged him in the ribs with the toe of his boot, but the man was out. He didn't budge. So Oscar grabbed him to his feet and shook him. The guy was all coat and bones, nothing more. Finally he came to, but could barely stand on his own. Oscar told him to beat it. The man mumbled he was too exhausted and bent back down to sleep. Oscar seized him by the collar and gave him a shove, but the old man couldn't keep his feet and hit the pavement face first. The blood leaked out of his head into a swelling puddle.

So far, his story matched the police report. Oscar recited the details of the murder with the same matter-of-fact callousness.

"He was bleeding all over the place. I freaked and ran."

"How'd they arrest you?"

"Later that night, I cruised into White Castle, drunk off my ass. There must've been an unmarked out front because two pigs in a booth watched me stagger in. I tried to be cool, knew I couldn't ditch right off. But they got up, and I ducked for the door. I tripped off the curb, and they nailed me. I never should've gone into that Castle. Stupid."

Carter scribbled notes on the form. Oscar stared out the window streaked by the wet snow. "When can I smoke, dude?"

Carter checked his watch. Mickey's big hand rested on the eight, his little hand between the three and four. The other kids would still be in group, so they couldn't use the lounge. Carter might have let him smoke in his office, but Judy would be all over the telltale smell. He glanced out the window at the snow. "You want a cigarette badly enough to smoke one outside?

"What's wrong with here?"

"The rules, you know. Technically, the entire hospital, building and grounds, is smoke-free—except for one lounge currently in use—but I think today, because of the, ah, circumstances of your arrival, we can make an exception if we go outside."

Oscar eyed Carter suspiciously, sizing up what might be expected in return. "Whatever."

They couldn't sneak out without Judy noticing. Carter told her he was giving Oscar a tour and marched out quickly before she could ask questions. Carter knew he could be in trouble like the time when he brought the kids back late from their A.A. meeting and Judy detected the Dairy Queen coffee cup that one of the kids still carried. She had asked Sister Mary Xavier if caffeine had recently been approved for the kids without the nurses knowing it. Sister X had put Carter on a week's probation for taking the kids to a location that the director hadn't approved in advance.

Carter led Oscar downstairs past Medical Records and out a back door behind the cafeteria. He sometimes used that door as a shortcut when he couldn't find a spot in the ramp and parked his car in the back lot. Even in this out-of-the-way location, he ran a risk. If word got back to Sister X that he let one of the kids smoke on hospital grounds, it would be at least a week's probation, probably worse.

They hunched beside the dumpsters where the thick snow gathered in gray puddles. Sneaking a cigarette reminded Carter of junior high school, when he and his buddies smoked outside the pool door between classes. Oscar, picking up on his nervous glances, cupped his cigarette in his hand between drags and said, "Dude. It's cool."

The admission paperwork called for a patient's drug history—they still had to justify his stay there. Carter figured this was a good time to start it.

Oscar surprised him by talking fairly openly about the drugs he had used, how often he had used them, where, and in what situations. Usually at the first interview, kids minimized the amount they used, thinking they still had a chance to avoid treatment. Other times, they exaggerated their past, boasting with junkie pride about gigantic quantities of drugs they had consumed. But Oscar spoke of his use neither in swaggering terms nor in understatements. He spoke in a realistic tone that let Carter know he had thought about drugs and was aware of how they had turned on him.

"When's the first time you got high?"

"High or drunk?"

"Either."

"Kindergarten."

He had snuck sips of adults' drinks and discovered the magic in them. In third grade, he got stoned for the first time on some pot he stole out of his mother's purse.

"That was better than drinking."

"Didn't make you sick?"

He dragged on his cigarette then said without letting out the smoke, "Felt better."

In fifth grade, he began running crack for the older kids, but never touched the stuff himself because he saw what it had done to them. In sixth grade, he discovered acid and began a love affair with it. "Everything makes sense when I trip."

The most he ever took was seventeen hits at a Grateful Dead concert two summers ago. He held up his right hand. "They told me I cut off my finger to experience what it would be like to be Jerry Garcia."

Carter shuddered.

"I didn't feel a thing—not even in the emergency room the next day."

Not long afterward, he tried ecstasy and thought it was the ideal drug. "X, when it works..." His eyes glittered. "Nothing better."

"What do you mean?"

"You want to screw everybody."

"What about afterward—the aches, the depression?"

"I've had worse hangovers."

"And when it doesn't work?"

"You want to fuck people over." He sucked on his third cigarette. "But I never lost a fight on X."

When ice came around, he liked that the high came quicker and more intense than with ecstasy.

"What else?"

"'Shrooms, coke, 'ludes—whatever was around."

About the only drug he had not taken was heroin. "I don't like needles, dude, but if it was that or nothing, I'd probably try it."

Carter leaned against the hospital's brick wall, out of the snow's way, but he could not escape its chill. Oscar finished his cigarette, snubbed it out against the wall, and placed it back in his pack. Talking seemed to have calmed him. His shoulders had softened some. When they got back upstairs in Carter's office—again hurrying by Judy before she could ask questions about Oscar's jacket and Carter's sweater being wet (she inhaled deeply and suspiciously at their passing)—

Oscar seemed almost willing to be there. He complied with the urine test and did not fight the obligatory strip search. He protested only with a silent grimace when Carter flushed the joint he found in Oscar's cigarette pack down the toilet. But it was too much for him when Carter told him the nurses would store his cigarettes.

"Thought you said this wasn't a fucking jail."

"I know it's a pain, but around here smoking is considered a privilege."

"Seems more a punishment to take away my cigs."

"The nurses will give them to you at scheduled smoking breaks."

"That sucks."

But he did surrender his pack.

Carter still had one more detail to arrange with Judy before he could turn Oscar over to her and finish the admission paperwork.

"I know we had talked about doing it differently, but I want to put Oscar with Rodney and move Archie to Chip's room."

Judy, perched behind the raised counter that marked the nurses' station, peered at Carter over her half-rimmed glasses with a look of pained annoyance that she might have directed toward a small boy at the beach who would not stop throwing sand in his sister's hair. Mid-forties, her age showed more in a general impression of poor health than in any particular feature. She had a small face, dotted by two beady eyes and lined by thin lips. A weak jaw gave her the appearance of an overbite, though her teeth lined up orderly. At the base of her neck grew a mushroom-shaped wart, the size of a fingernail, with a cauliflower texture. When Carter's eyes fell upon it, which was often—they seemed to be drawn to it—the wart repulsed him.

"My orders were to put the new admit in room 612 with Chip."

It was such a simple request; Carter hadn't expected a conflict. It further annoyed him that she insisted on referring to Oscar as "the new admit" when he stood right before her.

"I'm not here to give you orders—"

"Sounds to me like you're trying."

Sister Mary Xavier had routinely signed the order for Oscar to take the open bed in 612, probably without thinking about it. If Carter explained the situation to her, she would have taken his side, but he didn't want to make that much out of it. The problem was Judy considered a written instruction akin to a commandment.

"I'm merely suggesting that, for therapeutic reasons," this he underscored with raised eyebrows, "we place Oscar with someone who is further along in the program."

"I suppose you also consider smoking therapeutic?"

"Smoking?" Oscar said. Until that point, he had observed

the quibble with a silent, mocking smirk as though watching two parents argue over a point of complete indifference to him. "Who's smoking?"

Judy, startled, as though she had forgotten he was there, turned her look of annoyance on him while she said, "Nothing is as simple as you seem to think when you make your 'therapeutic suggestions,' Carter. Besides, Clarence is occupied at the moment."

As though that settled the matter, she returned to the entry she had been making in the chart opened before her. The cauliflower wart on her neck leered back at Carter. He wanted to pluck it off.

Just then, Buddha ambled out of the kitchen and lumbered toward the nurses' station slurping a strawberry shake from a plastic water bottle marked SlimFast, completely undisturbed by any pressing obligations. "Hey, Carter. Whaddya say?"

Judy sneered at him.

Unaffected by her look, Buddha, the recreational therapist, turned to Oscar and stuck out a meaty paw. "You must be the new kid on the block. Whaddya say?"

Oscar ignored the hand extended to him, ran his eyes up and down—and around—Buddha, then scowled at the beefy, open face smiling down on him.

Buddha withdrew his hand as calmly and as happily as if Oscar had pumped it with the joy of seeing an old friend and tugged a long slurp from his shake. His soft round body rested atop two enormous thighs the size of hundred-pound flour sacks that slumped together at the knees. When Buddha walked—waddled, actually—his thighs rubbed against each other emphatically. The shape of his round, brown face made him appear to be always smiling. Judy was the only one who called him by his given name, Clarence.

Carter appealed directly to him. "Buddha, do you have a moment to help Archie move his things into 612 and change the sheets on his bed in 610? We're going to place Oscar in 610 with Rodney."

Buddha took another enthusiastic slurp from his shake. "Sure, no problem."

Judy scribbled furiously in her chart.

Instead of feeling vindictive, Carter walked back to his office wondering if he had acted too impulsively in showing up Judy. He had achieved the desired result without considering the long-range implications. By the time he sat back down at his desk to finish the paperwork of Oscar's admission, he realized she had gotten the better of him again.

As he filled out Oscar's drug history, Carter had little doubt that the kid needed treatment. The question was whether Oscar would accept the help, or if he had survived on the streets for so long that he couldn't surrender.

Something else puzzled Carter: why Oscar had lied about

how he was arrested. The police report stated that Oscar had shown up at the emergency room of Saint Jude's, about seven blocks from the mission, with the old man on his back, shouting and screaming that the wino couldn't be dead. A police officer admitting a domestic violence victim arrested Oscar for his belligerence when the emergency staff's repeated efforts to quiet him failed. Later that night, Oscar confessed to killing the old man.

CHAPTER 2

The wet snow had greased the roads. The other drivers braked and jerked as though they had never driven in winter. Carter cursed them through the windshield. The six-mile commute to his apartment, which usually took ten minutes, took nearly an hour that evening. All the stops and starts on the highway must have taken their toll on his '82 Prelude because the engine rattled with a strange and probably malignant new symptom. By habit, he turned up the volume on the radio. Sting's new hit took over. He sang along on the chorus, "All this time the river flowed endlessly out to sea…"

Stuck in traffic, he felt like he was stuck at sea. His thoughts returned to work. That morning, when Sister Mary Xavier had entrusted him with Oscar's intake, she had told Carter how pleased she was with his work. His thoughts skipped past that moment to the conflict with Judy. By the time he pulled up to his apartment building, a knot gripped his shoulders.

He parked, checked the mail—a telephone bill and a

coupon for pizza delivery—and climbed the two flights to his apartment. Slipping the key in the lock, he felt a fleeting wish for someone on the other side to ask about his day.

After dinner—curried chicken reheated in the microwave, leftover from an immemorable date the previous Saturday night—he sought relief in a hot bath by candlelight. No sooner had he settled into the comforting warmth than the phone split the mood. He resisted the impulse of curiosity to get out of the tub and pick it up. The machine answered it on the third ring.

"Carter?"

Mom.

"It's Thursday night, March first. Remember March first?"

Damn. He had thought of it earlier in the week, jotted a reminder on his desk blotter to send a card, but the clutter of papers had obscured the note.

"Your brother called this evening, had Kelly Jr. sing 'Happy Birthday.' We didn't hear from you and wondered if something might be wrong. It's not like one of you boys to forget. With all that bad weather we hear you're having up there, we got worried. We thought maybe you'd gotten into an accident or something. I almost called the hospital to see if you'd had the sense to stay there and wait out the snow, but—"

Carter snapped off the machine. He trudged along the wet trail of carpet back to the tub.

She called back. He counted seventeen rings before she gave up. He braced himself for the phone to ring again. It didn't, but it might as well have. The expectation shattered the serenity he had sought in his bath.

Carter used to crawl into her bed to have her scratch his back. While his dad snored in the room next door, she ran her fingernails across his back and told him stories of the pretty little girl who grew up an orphan. She had never known her father. When she was two, her mother died of cancer, and she was placed in the local convent, where the Sisters of Mercy raised her. Sequestered in a small town, she knew she didn't want to be a nun. She liked boys. Summer afternoons she wandered the convent gardens and fantasized about living the glamorous life pictured in magazines. To wear a fur coat, have a purse for every outfit, a closet just for shoes; to go to dinner parties that did not start until eight, the theater, the symphony, her husband dashing in his black tie; lazy summer afternoons lounging at the country club pool, winters at the beach. Her hand would rest idly on Carter's back. As her dreams grew, so did her intolerance for the small town and convent. She still attended daily Mass, but she stopped going to the soda fountain, shunned school dances, and only dated boys with cars who could take her to the city.

When she was eighteen, she met a medical student doing his residency at the county hospital. He was not dashing, but he was stable and dependable and handsome enough. He could promise her the good life. She fell in love. For a period, while they lived in a five-bedroom, four-bath house in Edina, she was happy to watch her dreams spread out before her: the dinner parties, the country club, her two sons. Then, when Carter was three years old, his dad accepted a position at the Mayo Clinic. Rochester, another small town, reminded her too much of her childhood.

The rest, Carter had to fill in for himself. Somewhere after the move, probably not long after, the drinking escalated. He remembered coming home from school and learning to look for her cognac glass about the house as a predictor of the evening. Often, if the bottle itself was in plain view, she would fall asleep in the den before fixing supper. He would put out her cigarette left burning in the ashtray and take off her shoes. On those evenings, his dad made dinner in the microwave and told the boys to let her sleep, that she was worn out, but Carter could never figure out from what.

Some days when he came home from school, the house would smell of chocolate chip cookies baking in the oven and she would have two glasses of milk waiting on the table for the boys. She met them at the door and hugged them until they begged her to please let go so they could eat the cookies. But if the slightest thing went wrong, say Carter accidentally knocked over his glass, she might scream hysterically and disappear into the den, leaving the spilled milk to drip over the table's edge onto the kitchen floor.

Some evenings, she woke up in the den and argued with their dad. Carter would find her later sitting at her vanity, the top to her crystal decanter missing among the perfumes, her cheeks streaked with mascara.

"Don't cry, Mommy." She sniffs and hugs him. He can feel her cheek moist against his. Finally, the tears cease, and he leaves her alone with her decanter. He walks out of the bedroom feeling big and proud inside, the smudge of black on his cheek a badge of her love.

Seared into Carter's mind, more vivid than any memory, actually a feeling rather than a specific event, are those days when he is five years old and his older brother is away at school. He spends those days with her walking in the arboretum, among the fragrant stalks of flox, the colorful beds of azaleas, and the sweet-smelling honeysuckle vines, just he and his mom, alone together with the day all theirs. Carter climbs trees, but she is never far away, always watching him.

One day, while he waits for her to return from the restroom, he picks a bouquet of different colored roses, carefully snapping the stems. When she walks out, he pulls the bouquet from behind his back. "Here, Mommy."

She stoops to accept the bouquet. "Carter, I told you to wait for me here without moving."

He thinks at first he may have done something wrong. He had been afraid of it when he picked the flowers, knowing she wouldn't let him do that if she were watching. But when she smells the flowers and he sees a tear slip down her cheek, he forgets where one of the thorns had poked under his fingernail. He has made her happy.

She takes him up on a hill where they can see the many pretty colors of the valley below—poppy red, jonquil yellow, iris purple—and they lie down on the grass and watch the clouds float lazily from one side of the sky to the other. He feels as warm and full as the bright sun in the clear, blue sky.

For perhaps an hour, nestled in the water up to his chin, Carter involuntarily played thoughts of her through his mind. She wanted him to be more like Kelly, whom she referred to in small talk with other doctors' wives as the "ambitious one," not because he was happy, but because he inherited her drive. He went to Harvard on a hockey scholarship and stayed to finish law school. With his specialty in mergers and acquisitions, Kelly had profited handsomely from the eighties. Carter had other ambitions, though they were less clearly defined. He knew they had something to do with living freely, but he was not always clear about the free from what or free for what. The freedom he had first glimpsed in sobriety had somehow gotten away from him over the years. When he had been in treatment, the barriers had seemed so clear. Now that he had removed the alcohol and drugs, what held him back was more elusive.

He shivered. The water in the tub had chilled. He didn't want to call. By this hour she was probably blitzed. But he figured that talking to her might be the best way to get her off his mind.

She answered. His dad never did, even if he sat within arm's reach of the phone. "It's never for me," he said, and he was usually right.

"Hi, Mom."

"Where are you?"

"Just got home."

"They said you left the hospital hours ago."

"I stopped at the gym on the way home."

"There's something wrong with your machine. It cut me off then didn't answer when I called back. Did you get my message?"

She sounded coherent. He couldn't hear her smoking. Carter thought he might still be able to redeem himself. "No, I just walked in. I wanted to talk to Dad."

"He's here. We just finished some birthday cake. I wanted to eat out, but he said he was too tired, so what could I do? Fortunately Meyer's had an extra cake. He picked up some Chinese on the way home from the clinic."

How romantic. "May I talk to him?"

He heard the click of her lighter. "Are you angry with me?"

"No, Mom. I simply wanted to wish him a happy birthday."

"Well, you sure waited long enough to do so. It's almost over."

"Mom," he whined. He hated when it got to the point where he whined for her to stop. "May I please talk to Dad?"

"The doctor wants me to go in for some tests this week."

So that's why she called. She was often sick, not in a serious way, but usually with some minor condition that required a doctor's attention and excused her to submit herself to his care. That made her feel better.

"What for?"

He heard her inhale on her cigarette. "It's fairly routine," she said vaguely.

Probably a biopsy. Her own mother had died of cancer. She wouldn't say the word.

Some people grind their teeth. Carter chewed his tongue. When he didn't know what to say—or, worse, when he knew but couldn't bring himself to say it—he moved his molars up and down over his tongue, a motion that made it appear he was chewing gum. He found himself chewing his tongue now.

"May I speak to Dad?"

"You're angry with me?"

"No, Mom. I'll say a prayer that the tests turn out okay."

Silence, then his voice, weary but not angry. "Hi, Son."

Always "Son." Carter couldn't remember the last time his dad had called him by his name. Even with Kelly around, they were both "Son."

"Happy birthday, Dad."

"Oh, thanks. Not much to do about it, I guess."

Carter heard the newspaper rustle on the other end. Already at a loss for words. He groped for the mundane. "How'd you celebrate?"

"Hmm? Oh, the nurses baked me a cake, made me wear a silly hat and blow out candles. Chocolate, my favorite."

"Mom said you just finished cake there."

"Lemon."

He never stood up to her, but he always managed to make clear his annoyance. *Stay away from that.* "Have you taken out the Porsche yet?"

"No. Roads are clear of ice, but still too much salt and sand down."

A silver, mint condition '74 Targa was his baby. He moped in the winter when he had to drive a Mercedes 350 sedan.

"You'll be out there soon."

"Say, one of the nurses had this joke. Masochist says to the sadist, 'Tell me my faults.' Sadist says, 'No.'" Pause. "Masochist says, 'Tell me again.'"

He chortled. Carter gave him a courtesy laugh. "Not bad, Dad."

Silence weighted the line.

"So, what's the weather doing down there?" Carter asked.

"Steady rain. Snow's almost gone. Guy on TV says you've got rain mixed with snow."

"Mostly snow. Wouldn't be so bad if people would learn how to drive."

The newspaper rustled. Carter made an excuse about having to take something out of the oven, and his dad sounded relieved.

Later, Carter lay awake in bed staring into the darkness at the ceiling he couldn't see and listening to the couple in the apartment above his. He had never met either one of them but had come to know them through the sounds he overheard. Theirs was a faithful pattern of shouts, sometimes thuds, followed by her sobs. Finally, he listened to their bed grunt and groan with their love.

CHAPTER 3

After the noises upstairs had finally faded out—or Carter had become accustomed to the sound, the way people who live near tracks no longer hear the trains passing—he had fallen asleep. The phone woke him. Sister Mary Xavier.

The previous morning, she had summoned Carter to her office with a blue Post-It note on his door: See me. His first fear was that he had screwed up somehow. It was entirely possible that Sister X had received a complaint from an insurance company about his delinquent chart entries, though in the past she had praised his ability to stay a step ahead of the auditors.

He had knocked reluctantly at her office. The door was imposing: a large slab of carved walnut that depicted scenes from the life of the Virgin: the Annunciation, the Visitation, the Nativity, and so on. The door had once adorned the chapel sacristy of a convent in Italy. Sister Xavier had bought it at an auction. While Carter waited, he studied the carved figures of Mary and Jesus at the wedding at Cana.

He heard no reply. Perhaps she had not heard his knock. He rapped on the door again, louder. From within came the hiss of an aerosol can, the slam of a desk drawer, then Sister Xavier's sharp command, "Entrez!"

The interior of her corner office matched the splendor of its entrance: oil paintings on loan from the Walker Art Center lined two walls of cherry wainscoting; floor-to-ceiling windows on the other two walls filled her office with views of the river and university. She sat—or, rather, reigned—behind an enormous oak desk, framed by a high-backed leather chair. "Carter. Good morning. Coffee? Help yourself."

"Why not? Thank you." Carter pulled himself a cup from her antique brass espresso machine. He spied the ashtray tucked away on a lower shelf of her bookcase. The hairspray that hung in the air stung his eyes.

"Carter," she began before he had settled into the leather armchair opposite her. "As you know, Six West has struggled this past fiscal year."

She pressed her palm toward him. "I know you don't like those terms, but we must discuss business. My job is to make this unit profitable so you can keep yours."

My work is helping kids, it's not a business, he wanted to say. But he knew better than to talk back to Sister X.

"With insurance companies becoming more selective

in paying for residential treatment and the HMOs refusing altogether, we have to ask, who will pay? Private parties can't—too expensive. Charity beds are out—the hospital will give us no more for the balance of the year. So, who will pay?"

Carter shrugged, uncertain of what she wanted from him.

"I have been asking myself that question the past several months. Finally, I believe I have found the answer."

She leaned back against her leather chair and smiled for the first time since Carter had entered her office. Still thinking he might be in trouble without knowing it, he missed his cue.

When Sister Xavier smiled, you wouldn't call her pretty, but she had presence. She wore a tailored, power suit, reminiscent of earlier years when she had studied in Paris and developed her legendarily expensive tastes. Thursday morning's navy-blue suit shunned the contemporary shoulder pad fad, and probably rightly so—her broad shoulders already made her authentically imposing. Her frame was large yet not overweight, her face plain yet dignified. Whatever she lacked in physical handsomeness, however, she made up for with her powerful eyes: dark-blue beams that gripped you in their gaze and would not let go until they had finished their business with you.

When she had taken over as executive director of Six West two years ago, her first project had been the renovation of her office, once the staff conference room. When the hospital administration had challenged her proposal, she had stared them down with those powerful blue beams and said simply, "If you want me to transform this unit into a profitable business, you'll have to trust my decisions. Either you're with me, or you're in the way."

The other nuns of her order, the Sisters of Humility, stood by quietly, watching her with expectant pride. The only nun of the order with an MBA, Sister Mary Xavier's vocation was business. Five years earlier, she had taken over the order's sagging nursing home and miraculously turned it into a profitable venture for the nuns, primarily through fundraisers that preyed upon local parishioners' sympathetic generosity. Word was that, with the Mother Superior getting on in years, the order's thirty-two-year-old wunderkind was being groomed to take over.

In spite of Sister Xavier's contemporary fashion, she was one of the few remaining nuns who still wore a headpiece. Though not the wimple of medieval days, she wore one of seventies' vintage, with the cardboard frame atop the head and the trailing cloth that fell over her shoulders. Tipped back slightly on her forehead, it crowned a set of carefully coifed blonde curls. Her stately bearing and corporate decor demanded the respect due an executive, yet Carter could not help but approach Sister X with the reverence shown a nun.

His mother had indoctrinated him with this inflated

homage. They had been to the arboretum to see the first flowers of spring pushing their way through the soil: white and yellow crocuses and stalks of tulips with petals still balled like a baby's fist. On the way home, they had stopped at Saint Anne's Church to light a candle for Mary and say a prayer.

Coming in from the bright sunshine, Carter's eyes needed a moment to adjust to the dim lighting. Once they did, he became intrigued by a group of seven women cloistered before the tabernacle of the Blessed Sacrament. The women were cloaked in white and wore funny white hats that looked like cloth wigs. They murmured with their heads bent, forearms leaning on the pew in front of them, foreheads bent to clasped hands. Colored sunlight streaming through the stained glass lit their robes in a celestial glow that reminded Carter of the story when Jesus, Moses, and Elijah radiate before the disciples in a special light from heaven.

"Who were they?" Carter asks Mommy that evening when he crawls into her bed. His first impression of nuns—the image of the white-robed women bathed in bright light praying before the consecrated Eucharist—set in his memory like colors on a photographic plate.

"Nuns." She pronounces the word as though saying a prayer. "Brides of Christ."

She explains to him how the nun gives herself completely to Christ in a sacred union. Her body becomes a temple of prayer. "Nuns, like Mary, are blessed among women."

"Why aren't you a nun, Mommy?"

She does not say anything for what seems a long time. He can hear the snoring from the next room.

"Because I married your father." She laughs bitterly. "I can't say who got the better deal, those who live without or me living with him."

She laughs again, as though to wipe away the thought, and looks down at Carter lying next to her. She hugs him, brushing her hand through his hair. "They wanted me to be a nun, but I wanted to be your mother. Mary herself could not have loved her son more."

He hugs her back. "I'm going to be a priest and build a church and call it Saint Elizabeth's, all for you."

"The county!" Sister Xavier declared triumphantly.

"The county?" Carter repeated, shaken from his reverie.

"The county will pay for treatment where insurance companies and HMOs won't. I've known that for weeks, but it wasn't until yesterday that I was able to convince an old classmate of mine down in Juvenile how the county would benefit."

This time, Carter caught his cue. "How's that?"

She smiled, pleased. "Juveniles who successfully complete treatment spend less time in the courts, less time in corrections. The county spends less on them. Why not make an initial investment in a juvenile to save money in the long run?"

"They'll go along with it?" He was skeptical. It wasn't clear to him how he fit in her plan.

"That's where our jobs overlap," she said in a conspiratorial tone, seeming to read the question in his mind. "Barnes, my high school classmate from Holy Angels, still a dutiful Catholic, has finally agreed to send over a test case. He says this is a tough kid, doesn't think he'll make it. I want you to see that he does."

Carter blanched. You can't force a kid to recover. At best, a third of the kids who complete treatment stay straight. Another third eventually make it. The rest don't. Carter's role was simply to show the way. It was up to them, not him, to surrender and accept help. Ultimately, it was up to the grace of their Higher Power. When a kid did make it, Carter saw it as a miracle. Sister X was commissioning him to guarantee a miracle. He could not explain this to her. He could not even protest.

"I'll do my best."

"That's not good enough." She gripped him with her navy-blue eyes and said in a tone that made him believe more than his job depended on it, "See that he makes it."

Perhaps she read the apprehension in his expression because her tone softened. "I'm asking you to do this because the kids look up to you. They respect you for knowing what it's like, having been there yourself."

Yet, he thought, *sometimes they push me away for the same reason: they don't want to identify with me as a recovering addict.*

"One more thing: others aren't to know about this arrangement with the county. I want to see that it works first. So this is between us, understood?"

He nodded in mute agreement. She had secured him as her accomplice.

Then, that night, after the couple upstairs had worn themselves out and he had finally fallen asleep, she had awakened him with her phone call.

"Carter?"

"Mmm?"

"This is Sisser Savier."

"Yeah."

"What time is it?"

"Huh?"

"You were asleep. This is Sisser Savier."

"I know."

"See that he makes it."

"Sister?"

"See that he makes it, Carter."

"Yes, Sister."

"I knew you would."

CHAPTER 4

When Carter walked into the conference room the next morning for the Friday staff meeting, he found Dana and Howard sitting there, not speaking. Dana twisted the ring on his finger—Carter noted that the tiger's eye matched the stones in his bracelet—and Howard chomped on a toothpick. Dana greeted Carter then looked at his Rolex. Carter consulted Mickey. Two minutes early. He sat down and unwrapped the muffin that he had picked up at the hospital cafeteria downstairs. It seemed terribly misleading to call the hardened lump of dough with crunchy raisins "Morning Glory."

Dana watched him strip off the paper and made a peevish face, like a child confronted with a spoonful of cod liver oil. "Last night we had the most fabulous dinner," Dana said to Carter. "Have you dined at Cote d'Azur yet?"

Howard, who always walked into a room looking like he would rather be leaving, quietly chomped on his toothpick. Occasionally he reached to his nose to push back his black-rimmed glasses. Dana and Carter tacitly agreed to ignore him.

Carter knew of Cote d'Azur. The chic new restaurant downtown was the latest rave of food critics, and well out of his budget. He had smelled the wonderful aroma walking by on his way to Subway. Dana could pay his bill there without bothering to look at it.

"No, I haven't had the pleasure, yet." Carter used a gulp of coffee to help him chew the muffin. "Is that the new seafood joint in the warehouse district?"

Dana gasped. "Most certainly not. You must get out more often, lad."

For all of Dana's foibles, Carter liked him. He could be shrewd and petty, but he was basically well meaning. A recovering alcoholic himself, he had the kids' best interest at heart. He was the sort of doctor who listened first to the person then to the problem. There was no malice in his façade, something that the kids readily sensed, too. Still, Carter couldn't resist teasing him, he was so easy.

"I just thought with a name like that, you know, it would be a seafood joint with shrimp cocktail and catfish filets."

"Hardly. The cuisine is exquisite. We had an absolutely charming meal."

Judy entered the conference room, bumping the door open wider with her hip, her arms loaded with patient charts. Dana checked his Rolex. Carter pressed the muffin crumbs on the table and licked them off his fingertip, pretending not to notice Judy's struggle with the shifting pile of charts. She maneuvered the load to the table, but not before one chart dropped to the floor with a crash, spewing papers about her feet. She still managed a cheery, "Good morning, Doctor Donnelly."

Dana nodded.

Howard leaped to his feet, stumbling over his chair to help his wife collect the papers. In his haste, his glasses slipped off his nose, and he messed up the spilled papers while he fumbled for his thick lenses.

"Howard," Judy snapped and slapped at his hand. She handed him his glasses. "Go back to your seat."

Judy apologized to Dana for her tardiness. She took her place at the table next to him with still no word to Carter.

Howard removed his frayed toothpick, glanced around, then tugged a small cylinder case from his breast pocket, slid out a fresh toothpick, and tucked the used one inside. Before shutting the case, he offered a toothpick to Carter.

"No, thanks. I just ate."

Howard gave him a confused look, shrugged, and replaced the case in his pocket.

Nathalie walked in with a pot of coffee and cups. Her perfume bathed the room. "Morning. Coffee anyone?"

Carter was ready for a refill. "Where have you been

all my life?"

"Right behind you, looking for the ideal man."

"Pity you're farsighted."

Nathalie sat down and swished a stray strand of auburn hair from her forehead, tilting her head to expose a long line of smooth neck. Though the wrinkles at her eyes betrayed her age and the remnants of a difficult divorce, her eyes sparkled with youthful mischief. Her nose had a playful lift to it, and her lips seemed always on the verge of laughter. Carter got a good feeling simply looking at her.

"Howard, you need a light?" she asked.

He poked up his glasses defensively. "Best cure for cigarettes I can recommend."

"Except for the slivers. I dated a guy once who chewed toothpicks—was like kissing a splintered rail." She winked at Carter. "You ever have that problem, Judy."

Judy paused with her charts. "No, my dear. I've been happily married for eighteen years."

"Is that what you call it?" Nathalie shot back.

Buddha shuffled in, slurping his signature strawberry shake out of his SlimFast water bottle. Dana checked his Rolex. Taking the kids out for activities, Buddha faced the potential problem of their rowdiness, but he was strict, and they rarely tried to cross him. One of his responsibilities as rec therapist was to come in early on Friday mornings to check on the kids so the nurses could prepare the charts for the staff meeting. Yet he lumbered into the conference room as relaxed as if he had just risen from a sound night's sleep. "Morning everyone, whaddya say?"

He sat down next to Carter and thumped his back with one of his beefy paws. "Whaddya say, Carter?"

"Hi, Buddha. How're the kids?"

"Angels."

"Oscar?"

"Stewin' about something. Won't talk to me."

"Did he sleep through the night?"

"Was up most of it, they tell me, sittin' in the window. Wouldn't talk to nobody."

"Is it true he cut off his finger while tripping?" Dana asked.

"That's what he told me."

"Ouch," Nathalie said.

Buddha tugged at his shake.

Judy busied herself with the preparation of the charts, opening each to the page for the doctor's orders, and loudly stacking them in alphabetical order, the metal binders clanking against one another. "He's going to be trouble."

"Where'd he come from?" Dana asked.

Judy paused with the charts.

"He'd been living on the streets," Carter said.

"How'd he wind up here?"

"Officer Patterson brought him over from Juvenile."

"Yes, but who referred him?" Judy pressed.

"Why don't you ask Sister Xavier for the specifics?"

"I was just asking a question, Carter. Easy does it."

Mindy's arrival squelched the conversation. Dana even forgot to check his watch. She wore an orange suit with wide shoulders and a short skirt. An aqua bow barely softened her starched white blouse. The rest of the staff was dressed casually. Howard, the staff psychologist, who would have been her logical role model—except that he was Howard—wore green polyester slacks, a yellow checkered shirt, and a spotted turquoise clip-on tie. Judy always wore her white nurse's pants with white tennis shoes. That Friday, she had on a beige cardigan. Nathalie occasionally wore a skirt, but that morning wore khaki slacks, a loose cotton sweater, and lavender socks under her Birkenstocks. Buddha and Carter wore jeans, sweatshirts, and sneakers. Dana even had on jeans—Girbaud, today—and he never wore a tie to work.

The first week of her internship, Mindy had dressed in the fashion one might expect of a graduate student: Levi's, casual blouses, Gap pullovers, and, her first Friday, a gray Champion sweatshirt with "College of Saint Benedict" in red letters across her chest. Carter had asked, jokingly, why it was that they had named the all-women school after a man. "The women didn't name the school," she said. "The church *fathers* did. They were too threatened—as men still are today—of women with their own wills." *Oops.* Carter noted. *Sore spot.*

That may have been the reason she had taken to Carter. Not for his humor, but as a project. She corrected him whenever he used exclusive male pronouns and went out of her way to point out examples of significant achievement by women. She could rattle off names of women neglected by history the way a baseball trivia buff could recite batting averages.

"Good morning, everyone," she said in the tone of a chairperson addressing her board, completely unaware of her outfit's impact or the fact that she was late. "Ooh, Nathalie, would you please pass me that coffee pot?"

"Darling," Dana said. "That outfit is...stunning."

"Thank you."

"Not at all."

That was Mindy: she walked through life a step behind the beat of the conversation, unaware of her faux pas. She was mortally obsessed with what others thought of her, yet oblivious to their actual perceptions. Her perpetual expression was that of someone suddenly asking herself if she had remembered to turn off the iron.

She smiled clandestinely at Carter as though to ask if he, too, approved of her outfit, but he avoided her look by glancing at Nathalie, whose eyes giggled. Carter took a quick sip of coffee to hide his own snicker.

"Have you started?"

Dana grimaced and again checked his Rolex. Buddha slurped his shake. "Waitin' on Sister X."

"Oh, I see." Mindy plucked a cat hair from her jacket sleeve.

The conference room was a tight, windowless space barely large enough to accommodate a table that seated eight. In that claustrophobic condition, Dana's irritation infected the rest. The room buzzed with tension. He fidgeted with his ring, etched patterns in the rim of his Styrofoam cup with his thumbnail, regularly checked his "timepiece," then sighed. He occasionally looked to Nathalie with a didn't-I-tell-you expression. She shrugged in response. The rest of them were as impatient to begin. Sister Xavier was already fifteen minutes late, which was not altogether out of the ordinary, though she fined anyone else who was more than five minutes late to a staff meeting. Finally, Dana said, "Buddha, would you check her office and inform her that we are ready to begin?"

Buddha took a slow tug at his shake. "Don' think that's somethin' I wanna do."

Dana sighed and looked around the room. Carter shook his head. Mindy checked her mascara in a pocket mirror, Howard poked up his glasses, and Judy rearranged the charts.

"Dana, you go," Nathalie joked. "We'll save your place."

"Right," he said, and gave her another I-told-you-so look.

Suddenly, Sister Mary Xavier's presence dominated the

room. She strode purposefully and without apology to her seat at the head of the table opposite Dana. They waited with an electric silence for her to speak. To her left, Carter could smell the cigarette smoke on her navy-blue power suit.

She surveyed her expectant staff and announced abruptly, "Let's staff the patients. Who's first?"

"Archie," Judy said.

"Mine," Carter said. "Howard, do you have his test results?"

"They're in the chart, Carter," Judy said. "Oh, haven't you read it?"

"Howard?" Sister Xavier snapped.

He flinched. "The tests show no significant mental disorder, so I don't think a dual diagnosis is appropriate. His responses did show a slightly below average IQ, though I think Archie's learning difficulties in school are more the result of his preoccupation with others' attention than a learning disability, so EBD rather than LD, and probably ADD as well. Archie suffers from an acute need for others' approval, not altogether uncommon in adopted children, often manifested at this age, rooted in perhaps chronic fear of abandonment."

"Thanks, Howard. That along with what we heard in Archie's First Step and family history, show harmful involvement—"

"Would you call it chemical dependency?" Sister Xavier interrupted.

"I could." Then, noting her expression, Carter said, "I will."

Insurance would cover chemical dependency, nothing less, even though a kid could be destroying himself and those around him with his drug use. Sister Xavier did not care for the subtleties; her background was business, not chemical dependency. In her two years at Six West, her mission had been to lift the unit out of the red. Her critics—primarily Dana and Nathalie—attributed this to her lack of understanding of chemical dependency as a disease.

Dana liked to quip that Sister X had developed the one question assessment: "Do you have insurance?" But none of the staff criticized her openly. Last October, the then program director, Scott Anthony, made the mistake of challenging Sister Xavier at a Friday morning staff meeting. He argued that a kid who had not only used acid on the unit but sold hits to other patients should be kicked out and turned over to the police rather than simply "disciplined." Scott accused her of keeping the patient simply because he had good insurance. Staff sympathy had been with Scott, but that afternoon he was gone. It wasn't until a week later at the next staff meeting that Sister X announced that she would assume the position of the acting program director, presumably to save the expense of his salary, until Six West had been full for a continuous thirty days. The unit had not been full for one day in the past six months, nor had she interviewed any candidates for the position.

"Has anyone observed any unusual behavior in Archie this past week?" Carter asked.

"Has anyone observed any snow in Minnesota this winter?" Nathalie said.

"Let me rephrase that: any behavior unusual for Archie?"

"Ate a cigarette—butt and all—in front of Oscar yesterday afternoon," Buddha said.

"Wednesday, he was talking about playing 'Rocket Man' in the dryer of the laundry room," Mindy said, "but I don't think anything ever came of it."

"No, nothing that time," Judy said, "but later that evening he jumped on top of the counter at the nurses' station and kept chanting '*carpe diem.*' If given the chance, I would once again recommend against that movie."

"Any repercussions from that, his jumping on the counter, I mean," Carter asked.

"I gave him a day drop for being in an area where he didn't belong."

The kids earned privileges and received consequences on a level system with four levels and seven days to each level. One day's good behavior boosted them a day, seven days of good behavior earned them a new level, and any variety of negative behaviors cost them either a check (three checks in one day lowered them a day in their level rating), a day, or a level. The kids' level rating was displayed on a large whiteboard behind the nurses' station.

Nathalie and Carter—along with CareCorps counselors everywhere—complained that the system placed too much emphasis on the kids' behavior and served as a distraction from how well they worked the program, which meant, in the philosophy of Alcoholics Anonymous, surrendering to their powerlessness over chemicals and turning their lives over to the care of a Higher Power. The parent company, CareCorps, Inc., however, required franchises to adhere to its level system, so at Six West they were stuck with it.

"Anything else?"

"I have a question about the fundraiser," Mindy said. "Is attendance mandatory?"

A unanimous look of irritation passed over the faces of the rest of the staff, the reaction similar to that of a high school class toward the student who reminds the teacher that they were scheduled to take a quiz that day.

Though Six West had been losing money for the past two years, Saint Jude's, run by the Sisters of Humility, was not hurting—the unit's lease was secure. CareCorps, Inc., suffered the loss. Sister Xavier had conceived the fundraiser and put in months planning and organizing the one-hundred-dollar-per-plate dinner, dance, and auction for the unit. The CareCorps, Inc., executives thought the idea ingenious (a fundraiser for a profit-minded venture!) and she somehow sold it to the hospital administration (fundraiser for a profit-minded venture?) but the Six West staff bemoaned the concept out of her earshot. "Dishonest," Carter complained. "Shrewd," Buddha said. "Desperate," Nathalie. "Tacky," Dana. "An unnecessary obligation," unanimous.

Even Sister Xavier appeared annoyed with Mindy's question. "This is a significant event for Six West," she said. "Each and every one of you is invited and encouraged to be part of this special evening."

Mindy smiled slightly at Sister Xavier's response and reached inside her jacket to adjust a shoulder pad.

"I meant anything else about Archie," Carter said.

"Last night he pushed the shoppin' cart from the laundry room down the hall, callin' 'Bring out your dead,'" Buddha reported.

Carter was the only one who laughed.

"Bring out your dead?" Dana asked.

"Monty Python's *Holy Grail*."

"Is that on the banned list?" Mindy asked.

"Not yet," Judy said. "But I would recommend it, along with *Dead Poets Society*."

Carter had chosen both.

"I suppose next you will tell me they have therapeutic merits?"

"That's a debate for another time," Sister Xavier said. "Who's next?"

"Rodney."

"He's ready to graduate next week, probably Wednesday or Thursday," Nathalie said. "All he's got left to do is present his Fifth Step."

Rodney had arrived at Six West four weeks earlier from detox, sullen and broken, a kid who by fifteen seemed to have lost everything already: father, home, school, girlfriend, the desire to live. The second day of his stay, one of the nurses had caught him sniffing butane from a lighter he had smuggled in. Later that afternoon, Judy found him in the laundry room sniffing White Out that he had swiped from the receptionist's desk.

After several more days, a week, another week, Rodney gradually came to accept the chance of a better life. Looking around him in treatment, he—like Carter seven years earlier—decided he wanted what other sober people had. He was able to accept what they had to offer. The information from videos, lectures, and assignments sank in. He listened to the other kids talk, asked questions of the counselors. He started to make the connection that alcohol and getting high made his life worse, not better—as he had believed when he arrived—and came to understand the saying, "Alcohol and drugs taught me to fly but took away the sky." Eventually, he glimpsed the spiritual side of situations.

"That boy's goin' to make it," Buddha said.

The rest of the staff nodded. A kid like Rodney made them appreciate their jobs.

"Next?"

"Oscar," Judy snapped.

Sister Xavier looked to Carter with renewed interest. "How did that go?

"He's a tough kid, that's for sure, used to doing things his own way."

"Will he stay, or will he run the first chance he gets?"

"Hard to say, but he understands that treatment is a shorter stay than Juvenile."

"If that's the only reason he's here, get rid of him. I want him here only if you think he'll make it."

The image of sadness that had flickered in Oscar's eyes came to Carter's mind. "He knows he's losing the fight. It's a question of whether he's ready to throw in the towel."

"I saw that in him yesterday," Nathalie said. "This expression passed over his face when I asked him about his tattoo—have you seen it? The Grim Reaper on his shoulder?—a convulsion of spontaneous grief, but it was gone in an instant. You know what he said? 'That's my dad, Father Christmas.' When I pressed him, his eyes flattened and he said, 'You shrink types ask too many questions.'"

Judy paused with the charts. "That boy's going to be trouble," she said to Sister Xavier. "Yesterday evening he was walking down the girls' corridor. I told him it was off limits. He kept walking to Whitney's room. I told him it was a day drop for a boy to be in a girl's room. He gave me such a hateful look and said, 'I haven't got a day to drop,' then walked right in."

"He'll have to earn that day back," Mindy said and looked to Sister X, her grin asking, *Isn't that right*?

Judy turned toward Carter. "If we bend the rules for him, he will think they don't apply to him."

"He knows he has to follow the rules. I explained them to him yesterday."

"Actions speak louder than words."

"He's going to challenge everyone, Judy," Nathalie said. "Don't let him snag you into a power struggle."

"Carter set up this power struggle."

"What are you saying, Judy?" Sister Xavier asked.

"That we cannot make exceptions for Oscar."

"Of course not."

Judy shot Carter a gotcha look.

To Carter, Sister X said, "Keep me posted."

"I'll finish his drug history today and get him started on the First Step," he said. "We'll get the psychological test results Tuesday, right Howard?"

"And urinalysis results from admission Monday," Judy said. "Nothing's changed, Carter."

He tried to ignore her. "I have calls in to his p.o. and his mother to collect more background."

"Good. Who's next?"

"Whitney."

"Mine," Nathalie said and was silent a moment, collecting her thoughts. "It wouldn't surprise me if Oscar already had sex with her."

Whitney Palmer was thirteen but precocious, accustomed to hanging out with kids much older. She took whatever drugs they gave her—acid, ecstasy, cocaine—and loved them. Mostly, she drank alcohol she stole from the 7-Eleven near her house in Edina. With natural red hair and makeup maturely applied, she already possessed a sultriness that no man could deny.

"With that sneaky little ginger?" Dana asked.

Well, almost no man. It did not surprise Carter that she had already been flirting with Oscar.

Nathalie nodded, her lips pressed together. "I think we've got incest with Dad here."

"Stan Palmer?" Mindy asked, her mouth staying open.

Carter thought he saw Sister Xavier wince.

"What are you basing that on?" her voice strained.

"I don't have anything definite, yet. But she dropped several hints during her First Step. And the behavior is all there."

"Several hints? Of a secret?" Sister Xavier's neck reddened. "That could be anything. She shoplifted her Gucci purse. She took out the parents' car. She had a crush on the paperboy. And you're saying that the hospital's chief administrator fondled her? Do you have any idea how serious that allegation is? You better have a lot more than *hints of a secret* before you start hurling accusations that could destroy us."

Nathalie remained calm. Not passively, but peacefully. Carter could see her counting her breaths. After a moment, she said. "The outward signs are there, though you're right that I couldn't prove it. Right now I'm going on intuition."

"Intuition?! Will your intuition defend this unit against a lawsuit? Is your intuition enough to destroy a man's reputation?" Sister Xavier could barely contain herself in her chair. "Let me tell you something. We will not discuss this subject again with Whitney. We treat chemical dependency here. We do not investigate sexual abuse. You will not hint at the subject or say anything that would encourage her to think of the possibility. Drop it."

She paused for a moment to catch her breath, then swept the room with her glare, and said in a lowered, even tone, "The rest of you heard nothing of the matter. When you leave here, the intuitions and intimations of this morning's discussion are forgotten. Do I make myself perfectly clear?"

The staff consented silently. Sister Xavier leaned back in

her chair, her thumbs massaging her temples just beneath the crown of her habit. "Next?"

They discussed the rest of the kids, twelve altogether, briefly reviewing the week's progress—or lack thereof—and briskly proposing the coming week's plan. Judy snapped the last chart shut, and Sister Xavier started to push herself away from the table. It had been at least an hour since her last cigarette—about forty-five minutes longer than she liked. The staff meeting was an endurance event for her. For the last fifteen minutes, Carter had watched her fidget with a stir straw she had plucked from the tray of coffee condiments.

"Did I tell you about my dinner last night?" Dana asked.

Sister Xavier paused, tapping her stir straw on the table.

"Poached sea bass baked *aux feuilles*."

"That will be all."

"But you should hear. We commenced with the *escargot au beurre, ensuite soupe de crevette*..."

Sister Xavier twisted the stir straw.

"*Ensuite le poisson, une assiette de fromage*..."

Sister Xavier twisted the straw into a knot.

"*Enfin, la pièce de résistance, une tarte aux pêches. Oh mon dieu—extraordinaire*!"

The straw snapped between her fingers.

"Of course, I could not tell you the quality of the wine, not having tasted it myself..."

Sister Xavier's fist slammed the table. "Meeting adjourned."

"But the *food* was exquisite."

CHAPTER 5

"She hadn't seen him?"

"They sat at opposite ends of the restaurant," Nathalie said between bites of the daily special: cucumber and cashew on seven grain. "He saw her come in; she didn't see him. He watched her get sloshed."

Sister Xavier's late-night phone call came back to Carter. He reached for his coffee. Outside the window, snow dripped from the sky. Its slush spread across the sidewalks and street. He watched a procession of unsuspecting pedestrians, one after the other, pick their way along the boulevard, trying to avoid the puddles on the sidewalk, only to be drenched by the spray from passing cars.

Carter and Nathalie usually walked the two blocks to Saint Phoenix, but that Friday, because of the wet snow, they drove. Carter's car still rattled, worse than the day before. Nathalie couldn't identify the noise either. She suggested he bring it into the shop.

Carter wrapped his hands around his mug and sipped the comfort of hot coffee. When he and Nathalie had arrived, Rosy had delivered their mugs, Nathalie's with two teaspoons of sugar, Carter's black. Customers brought in their own mugs and left them on the racks that hung between the dining room and the kitchen. Over the years, the racks had accumulated hundreds of mugs, resembling the wall of crutches at the Lourdes shrine.

Saint Phoenix, an old stone church built over a hundred years ago, had parquet floors and wooden pews converted to cushioned booths set between tall, arched windows. It took its name from the ceiling fresco of an enormous phoenix rising out of its ashes. The diner had opened its doors ten years earlier, on June 10, the date back in 1935 when Bill Wilson, an alcoholic struggling to stay sober, nursed Doctor Bob, another alcoholic struggling to stay sober, through a hangover. Old-timers of Alcoholics Anonymous passed on the story of how Bill W., who craved a drink while on a business trip to Akron, discovered the key to his sobriety was helping another alcoholic. Doctor Bob soon made the same discovery. For both of them, nothing else had worked. The fellowship of Alcoholics Anonymous was born out of the mutual support and understanding they found in each other that day. Framed portraits of the two founders were affixed inside Saint Phoenix astride the former church's front doors.

The Twelve Steps, stamped on wooden plaques, lined the walls on either side of the restaurant where the Stations of the Cross had once hung.

What had begun as a sober coffee shop, the recovering alcoholic's alternative to Denny's, had become a haven for a garden variety of recovery junkies. The A.A. meetings in the basement had gradually expanded to Narcotics Anonymous meetings. Then came Al-Anon and Adult Children of Alcoholics. Later, Overeaters Anonymous, Gamblers Anonymous, Emotions Anonymous, Fundamentalists Anonymous. And so on, until Saint Phoenix housed meetings around the clock of varied support groups with their own version of the Twelve Steps tailored to address problems from compulsive spending to living with a PMS-afflicted spouse. The most recent group forming—Carter had spotted the notice posted on the bulletin board at the entrance—was for elderly people with incontinence issues, called Dry Pride.

As demand for the limited space increased, Saint Phoenix raised the rent downstairs, which had forced several of the original A.A. groups to move to other meeting spots. About that time, the gift shop opened where the sacristy used to be. The shop sold self-help books and cassettes, medallions, daily meditation calendars, Bill W. refrigerator magnets, bumper stickers, and dish towels embroidered with slogans. Carter considered their presence irreverent—recovery was more than drinking herbal tea and wearing a T-shirt silk-screened with the Serenity Prayer.

Carter drained the last sip of his coffee and raised his empty mug—embossed with Edvard Munch's *The Scream*—to signal Rosy.

"Dana called me this morning," Nathalie said. "He counted three bottles of wine delivered to their table."

"*Their* table?"

Rosy came by with the coffee pot.

"Half a cup, please," Carter said.

Nathalie pushed forward her mug inscribed with the Japanese character for serenity. "I'll take the other half."

After Rosy had left, Nathalie continued her story. "She started kissing the waiters and he, the man she was with, laughed hysterically. Like a 'hyena in heat,' Dana said. She called for the chef. The maître d' came over, but she insisted upon seeing the chef. He finally came out, wiping his hands on his apron, expecting a complaint. Sister X wobbled out of her chair, tossed back her habit, and planted a wet one right on his lips. The chef was so befuddled that he ran back into the kitchen without a word. Sister X's date fell off his chair laughing."

She must have called him afterward. "Dana witnessed all of this?"

"The whole restaurant did. Dana was beside himself this

morning. He insists that we do something."

"Like what he did this morning?"

"Think about what she's doing to the unit. You've got to admit her reputation is hurting us."

"Yet she's still well-connected. Check out the guest list for her fundraiser."

"That's just it. Other treatment centers aren't resorting to fundraisers."

"True. You going?"

"Sounded this morning like we don't have a choice."

Losing a Saturday night, hearing of Sister X's escapade, and morning group with the kids had wearied Carter. Already it had been a long day.

After the staff meeting, the morning had started rather routinely for the kids. Rodney and Whitney argued over the television channel, Whitney in favor of *The Today Show* ("Bryant Gumbel is so cute"), Rodney wanting cartoons. They both turned against Chip when he blasted his Doors tape on the boom box. Archie sat by himself but managed to get teased for pouring orange juice over his Frosted Flakes. The other kids played their perpetual game of Monopoly. Oscar tipped his chair back against the wall, folded his arms across the chest of his jean jacket, and keenly observed the whole scene, detached, yet somehow intimately involved.

Chip was scheduled to present his First Step to the group.

The book *Alcoholics Anonymous*, the Bible of A.A., makes reference to "self-will run riot." That was Chip. In sixth grade, he started drinking wine smuggled from his parents' cellar. By junior high he was drinking daily. When he started getting into trouble, his father, an attorney, bailed him out each time, until Chip's friends trashed the house while his parents were in Europe. When his parents returned, they deposited Chip at Six West. It was clear to everyone that he was powerless over alcohol, that drinking had made his life unmanageable.

Everyone but Chip. "You're making too much of it, just like my parents."

"Getting expelled from three prep schools?"

"They had no sense of humor."

"Being kicked off the soccer team?"

"I would've said that to the coach even if I wasn't drunk."

"Getting arrested for possession?"

"They dropped the charges."

"Ticketed for DWI?"

"That cop was out to get me—no one else in the car got a ticket."

"No one else was driving."

"I got out of it anyway."

"What about rolling your dad's Range Rover?"

"How was I to know there was ice on the ramp?"

The other kids tired of his rationalizations. Even Archie

tried to make sense to Chip. "It's like you're banging your head against a brick wall and you're cutting yourself up, but you don't believe it will feel better to stop because you can't see the blood on your face."

"At least I haven't guzzled gas imitating a flamethrower, like you, No-Brain.

"Yet."

"I haven't had sex with slime just to get a joint, like our tramp Whitney."

"Yet.

"I haven't sold crack like Dirt here—what is your name, anyway?"

"Yet."

Chip turned to Carter. "What's with this 'yet' shit?"

"You haven't done those things yet. Keep drinking and you will."

Chip sneered at Oscar. "I'll never turn out like that." He flippantly tossed his blank First Step booklet on the floor in front of the group and announced, "I'm not powerless. I can quit anytime I want. I just don't want to."

The other kids had had enough.

"You idiot, don't you get it?"

"You're no better than the rest of us."

"That's your disease talking."

"Quit wasting our time."

"Get serious."

"Get real."

"Dude, you don't belong here," Oscar said in his gruff, cigarette-scratched voice, arms still folded across his chest.

"Thank you. You're a little dirty but not so dumb. That's what I've been trying to tell them. Did you hear that, Carter? Nathalie? I don't belong here. What will it take? Do I have to jump up and down on the table and—"

Oscar's gaze stopped Chip mid-rant the way a choke collar snaps a dog to attention. "You belong in a coffin." He leaned forward, "Keep calling me 'Dirt,' and I'll put you there quicker than alcohol can."

Thinking back on the morning, Carter sipped his coffee. "He understands the First Step."

"Dana?"

"No. Sorry. I was thinking about Oscar."

"He sure put it to Chip. Think it'll help?"

"Truthfully?"

"No, make something up to amuse me."

"I don't think Chip's ready to listen to others."

"Speaking of not listening to others, how about the way Sister X jumped on me at staffing?"

"Have you crossed her lately?"

"Not that I know of." Nathalie rubbed the tip of her finger across the serenity character on her mug. "Her reaction makes me think she's got something to hide."

"Like she's a victim herself?"

"Could be."

"The signs are there: 'We won't talk about it.' Your intuition terrified her. You got too close to the secret."

"So she had to attack me to dismiss my intuition?"

"Exactly."

"I'm not sure." Nathalie swirled the coffee in her mug. "I think it's something else."

She said it in a mysterious way, holding something out of Carter's reach. In a way that said she knew something about Sister Xavier that she could only know as a woman, clues that she had picked up that were foreign to a man. Carter could not get her to say more.

CHAPTER 6

"Oscar's in there," Judy said to Carter when he returned from lunch. "I told him that he would get another day drop, but he walked right in."

Carter noticed on the level board behind Judy that Oscar stood at minus two. "I'll talk to him."

"Sister Mary Xavier says no exceptions."

"Treatment is more than giving day drops."

"Don't enable him."

"I'll talk to him."

He reached for the handle.

"Your mother called. She wants you to call her back."

"She say anything else?"

He figured if she had heard negative test results, she would've told Judy.

"Just that you are to call her back."

That, he decided, could wait until the weekend.

Oscar watched Carter walk in. He sat, arms folded across

his jean jacket, in Carter's desk chair.

"Someone's been eating my porridge." His expression didn't change. "Sit down."

"Simon didn't say."

Oscar held up a familiar metal binder. "What's this?"

Carter sat down. "Your chart. Every patient has one. My question is how did you get a hold of it?"

Judy and the other nurses guarded the charts behind the nurses' station. They did not like to let the metal binders out of their sight. Even as a counselor, Carter had to negotiate at length with them to take one into his office. Inside the chart, Oscar would've found Carter's notes, Officer Patterson's report, Dana's report, and other sensitive impressions. Carter felt paradoxically betrayed and exposed. He promised the kids confidentiality, yet now Oscar had read his breach to the insurance companies.

Oscar flipped open the chart. "'Cut off finger under the influence of LSD—possible trigger of violent psychotic tendencies... Claims no family affiliation: last contact with mother six months ago, father absent... Probable abandonment issues.' Who reads this shit?"

"The staff. Insurance companies. Auditors. Not patients," he added defensively. "Unless they're eighteen or have a signed request from a parent."

Oscar scoffed. "'Preliminary diagnosis: chemical dependency.'

After one conversation? What the fuck?"

"You show symptoms of the disease."

"*Disease*? This is too much."

"Chemical dependency. It's a disease. With identifiable symptoms. You show several: increased tolerance, blackouts, failed attempts to quit—"

"Give me a fucking break."

"Have you read any of what I gave you yesterday?"

"I don't belong here."

"That's what Chip said."

"Fuck your mind games. I want out."

"All right." Carter reached for the phone. "I'll call Officer Patterson and have him come pick you up."

Oscar slammed his hand down on the phone. "Don't threaten me."

Carter flinched, instantly angry at himself for doing so.

"Where do you get off writing this shit about me?"

"You saw me taking notes."

Oscar yanked out the pages Carter had written and tore them into shreds. "You bastard."

Speechless, Carter watched Oscar walk out and slam the door. In his wake lay the pages Carter had carefully drafted the day before, torn and scattered across the orange carpet.

•••

Mickey's little hand had already swung past the six and reached toward seven, but Carter still hadn't finished rewriting Oscar's chart entries. He worried about what Sister Xavier would say if her test case bolted that weekend. If he alerted her of the possibility and Oscar did run, she might see it less as Carter's fault. But if he didn't run, Carter's warning would appear to her an acceptance of defeat, an admission that he had been unworthy of her confidence. Might as well not say anything. He gave Oscar the weekend to get over it, perhaps to adjust. Sometimes that was all it took for kids: a weekend with the other kids to get used to the place.

Carter knew he was trying to pull one over on himself, but he let himself believe it to dodge any further confrontation—at least until Monday.

He leaned back in his chair and stretched his arms over his head. A knot snagged in his shoulders. He needed a break.

He found the kids in the group room working on their craft projects. Usually Buddha took them outside to play in the snow or take walks, but because of the miserable weather that day, they spent their recreational therapy time inside working with clay.

Chip fashioned a crude spittoon.

"Who's that for?"

"Me."

"I thought you didn't chew."

"Who said that?"

"You did. That's what you and your soccer coach argued about."

"Like I'm going to tell him."

Rodney sculpted a pyramid with three sides. He had pushed up the sleeves of his brown suede, fringed jacket past his elbows. At the base of each side, he had spelled out the words of the A.A. slogan HOW: "Honesty, Openness, Willingness." "I wanted to bring part of this place home with me," he said.

"Be sure to sign it. Your name belongs with those qualities."

"Thanks, Carter," he said solemnly.

Whitney shaped a round dish and top that looked like two ashtrays. She told Carter it was for her diaphragm. "Those plastic cases are so flimsy."

Carter wished he hadn't asked.

Archie greeted Carter in his favorite Monty Python voice, a high falsetto.

Carter played along. "Been shopping?"

"No, been shopping."

"What'd you buy?"

"I bought an engine."

"What are you going to do with an engine?"

"I'm going to cook it."

"You can't cook an engine."

"Well, you can't eat it raw."

Carter laughed and tousled his hair. Archie worked diligently on a bust of himself with an unmistakable likeness. He had been working on the sculpture patiently for the two weeks he had been at Six West, and it revealed a natural talent. Carter complimented him on his progress. "It's no good," Archie said, but Carter could see him smile inwardly at the praise. Some of the other staff had little patience for Archie, but Carter felt an affinity toward him through his humor.

The rest of the kids molded standard items: ashtrays, vases, mugs, and so on. Except for Oscar. He sat in the corner, chair tipped back, arms folded across his jean jacket, in what had become his classic pose.

"Told him sometimes doin' nothin' is the best recreation there is," Buddha said.

The time with the kids refreshed Carter. Sometimes, lost in the paperwork, he forgot what his job was about. They reminded him why he was there.

On his way out of the group room, he nearly ran into Judy.

"There you are," she said.

"Wherever you go…"

"Your mother's here. I couldn't find you."

Carter's mom stood at the counter of the nurses' station. The sight of her produced an enormous feeling within him. She squinted at him down the hall the same way she had squinted into the sun in front of the beauty salon.

The pungent smell of Russian olive trees spreads through the car's open window where Carter waits across the street. Parked on a side road, just off Main Street, he faces the clump of olive trees on the corner and watches the Saturday morning traffic: several cars and a few pedestrians, mostly headed to the post office up the hill.

There had been an argument—Carter doesn't remember the content. Afterward, she had made Dad take her to the salon. Carter had smelled the cognac when she leaned over his cereal bowl to kiss him goodbye. Turning to kiss her, he caught a smudge of mascara under her cheekbone that she had missed. He knew she would spot it at the salon. Seeing the blemish in the mirror would give her anger at Dad a second wind. But Carter dared not point it out himself.

She would have made Dad drive her home, too, but Carter had lied that he was going that way later anyway and offered to pick her up. "Don't keep me waiting," she had said. He arrives ten minutes early, time enough to smoke a few hits.

He knows he will hear her side of the argument when she comes out. It is always Dad's fault, she says, usually because of his over-involvement at the hospital—or her perception of such, forgetting that his involvement there is what makes possible her annual trips to Hawaii, her fur coat, her new pearl necklace, and all the rest, even her weekly treatments at the salon. The more Carter hears her complain about Dad, the more he resists blaming him, and the more he figures it must be her fault. He stuffs a pinch of pot into his one-hitter and smokes it quickly, the slim brass tube discretely tucked into his palm.

He spots a figure in crumpled clothes with a wild beard emerging from behind the clump of Russian olive trees: Rocky. His shuffling, unsteady gait makes him appear drunk, but as he hobbles closer, his limp comes into clearer focus. Rocky shifts his bad foot, a stiff lump of a shoe, ahead of him, sways, and hurries his good leg around to catch himself from lurching forward. With each effort, his face growls in pain. He probably is drunk—he usually is—but not enough to ease the pain of the bad foot he rakes down the sidewalk.

Carter knows Rocky the way everyone else does, from having seen him panhandling the daily Mass crowd or climbing out of the Salvation Army box behind the shopping mall. Someone dubbed him Rocky, short for Rockefeller—no one knows his real name. The story is that he had been a brilliant young scientist who fried his mind with too many laboratory drugs: LSD, STP, XTC, etc. He crippled the foot later.

But this morning, seeing Rocky grimace as he tromps past the beauty salon, Carter sees him as someone who once had been a little boy, someone who dreamed about what he would be when he grew up, someone who had fallen in love with a young woman, yet someone whose life over the years has been reduced to a limp. Carter smokes another hit.

Just as Rocky passes the door of the salon, Mom appears. She shields her eyes from the sun, spots Carter, and motions him to the curb. She stands not five feet from Rocky, unaware of—or ignoring—him. She stands tall, palm cupped to her forehead, saluting the world freshly coifed. Carter loses sight of Rocky and sees only her, the sunlight dazzling in her hair. An irresistible feeling of love for her comes over him and smothers all of his earlier feelings.

This feeling swam through Carter as he approached his mom squinting at him from the nurses' station. For many women her age, their early twenties were buried in their face by their forties. You had to search their features to find the good looks that once presided there. Not so with his mother. The years had deepened her good looks, made her beauty even more distinctive. Her face radiated not only beauty but character. The face he remembers, anyway.

But this evening, he saw that the sickness had overwhelmed her good looks. Her perpetual tan had paled. An unnatural yellow had crept into the edges of her eyes. The salon's best makeup could not conceal the wearied expression that clung to her face. Her appearance inspired a sudden distaste in him. Instead of kissing her on the lips she offered him, Carter gave her a peck on the cheek.

"Carter." She took his face in her hands and kissed him on

the lips. Her breath was clear, but her hands felt cool and damp.

"What a surprise."

"Didn't you get my message?"

"I told him you called," Judy said.

They went into his office.

"Let's have dinner," she said. "My treat."

"I'd like to, but I've got some work left to finish. I can take a break to have coffee with you."

Friday nights, Carter played hockey in a men's league, but he didn't want to bring that up with her. If they just had coffee, he might still be able to make his game.

She gave him a pouting look.

"What brings you up here?"

She stuck her finger into the pot of one of his plants. "Needs water."

"Did you get your test results?"

She slipped a cigarette from her purse, still not saying anything, and put it in her lips. She looked to Carter, waiting for a light.

"Sorry, Mom. The hospital is smoke-free."

"Oh, Jesus. Of course it is."

Her face looked old and torn when she cursed.

"Let's go have a coffee. There's a place down the street."

On the way to the car, a coughing fit overcame her. The coughs racked her chest with a wicked grating, like a dull saw against bone. She leaned against one of the ramp's concrete pillars. He watched helplessly.

When she finally caught her breath, she lit a cigarette and sucked on it for relief.

"My car's this way."

The Prelude limped the two blocks to Saint Phoenix. She didn't say anything about its horrible rattle. Carter didn't mention it either.

Rosy brought Carter his coffee. "For you, ma'am?"

"Bring me a Courvoisier on the rocks."

"Excuse me?"

Carter felt his cheeks flush with embarrassment.

"Courvoisier, with ice. And an ashtray," she added, glancing around the table.

"I'm sorry, ma'am. We don't serve alcohol."

"All right then," she said, annoyed, the ash on her cigarette growing longer. "I'll have a glass of your house white."

Rosy gave Carter a look of appeal.

"Mom, they don't serve alcohol."

"I heard him, Carter. Make that a zinfandel."

Rosy had become amused. Carter could see him trying to hold back the grin pulling at the corners of his mouth. His embarrassment deepened to rage.

"Mom, order something without alcohol."

"Don't use that tone with me."

"Bring her coffee with cream."

"I'll have tea, Earl Grey."

"That I can do," Rosy said and trotted off, giggling to himself.

His mother flicked the ash of her cigarette on the hardwood floor. "Why did you bring me here, of all places?"

"I always come here," Carter said weakly.

They sat for a spell without words. She took in the framed portraits astride the door, the Step plaques along the walls, and finally the phoenix rising above them. In the squint of her expression, he could hear her describing it to her book club: "Then this gigantic...winged monster on the ceiling—I've never seen such a tasteless interior!"

Carter recognized several people heading downstairs for the 7:30 A.A. meeting and nodded. Buddha was one of them. Seeing Carter, he came over to the table.

"Mom, do you remember Buddha?"

Buddha shifted his strawberry shake to his left hand and stuck out his right hand. "Pleasure to see you again, Mrs. Kirchner."

"And you."

"Carter giving you all the latest gossip?"

"I would be the last to listen."

"A fine lady, Carter. You couldn't do better."

He shuffled over to the counter. They watched him pay for a carob brownie and head downstairs.

"That boy could stand a diet."

"We all have our weaknesses."

Before she could respond, another coughing fit ambushed her. The coughs grated against her chest in merciless spasms. Several people at the tables nearby turned at her hacking, sympathetic expressions on their faces. Rosy brought over a carafe of water, but she waved him off. Her eyes strained and her face twisted with the effort of her coughs.

When she finally appeared over the fit and had wiped the moisture from her eyes, Carter wanted less than ever to ask. Now that the question held such weight—it was no longer polite conversation—he wanted to run from it.

"They wanted me to come up here for more tests," she said.

"They can't do them at Mayo?"

"There's a specialist here."

"For what?"

"They wouldn't say." Or she wouldn't.

"How long have you had this cough?"

She waved her hand. "They know what that is: bronchitis."

"Then what are the tests for?"

"I don't like to talk about it." Her tone added, *I won't talk about it now.*

She squinted at him through her headache. He saw in her pain the sad little orphan girl the nuns had adopted. He remembered his own childhood promise to build her a church.

She reached for a cigarette, waited for him to light it.

"Mom, do you really want another one?"

She clamped the cigarette in her lips defiantly. "Don't start your counselor crap on me, Carter."

He lit her cigarette and watched her inhale with a sinking feeling.

CHAPTER 7

Carter returned to the unit, finished redoing Oscar's chart, and said good night to the kids. He had missed his game. He drove home through the snow in a daze. The vision of his mom's sickness hung before him.

The flakes had changed to the same wet heavy snow of that night in Montana. They are at Red Lodge, where the family skis over the Easter holiday. This year, he can ski down the blue square slopes, though he still shies away from the black diamonds because they make you go so fast that when you fall you don't stop but keep sliding and can lose a pole or hat or ski. There is a man Carter remembers from the year before. He seemed to be a nice man because he made Mommy laugh. The man has a loud voice and a deep laugh. They sit together—Mommy and the nice man—in the part of the chalet where only grownups are allowed to sit and laugh so that Carter can hear them from across the great room. Daddy never goes into that part of the chalet. The man with the loud laugh is a big man, much bigger than Daddy, and younger, too. Carter had not noticed that last year, but this year, now six years old, he has started to distinguish such details and to make comparisons. He prides himself on this. The man is definitely bigger than Daddy.

It's evening, after dinner, though not late because Carter is not yet in his pj's. They are in the chalet: Daddy, Kelly, and Carter, with some other skiers—five or six grownups who play a game of cards at a corner table. Daddy reads one of his books, Kelly tries to learn a new trick with his yo-yo, and Carter plays with a hook-and-ladder fire engine. It's a shiny red engine with a long white ladder that extends as long as his arm by turning a small metal wheel the size of a half dollar. The television is switched on, and its noise fills the room.

Mommy and the big man walk over to where the rest of the family is, not straight toward them but in an indirect sort of way. Mommy laughs a little more than usual and looks like she might be dizzy. She has her hand through the big man's elbow. Daddy has noticed them. He hasn't moved his head or anything, hasn't shown that he noticed them, but Carter sees his eyes sneak a look at them for an instant then retreat back to his book. Daddy doesn't look up, even when the two of them stand in front of him. They aren't laughing loudly anymore, but Mommy still giggles a little bit. Up close she looks even dizzier. And she still hangs on to the man's elbow. Carter has seen her like that somewhere before, but where was it?

"Must be a good book," Mommy says.

Daddy does not look up.

When Mommy isn't talking, no one else in the room is talking. The group playing cards tries to look at their cards but can't help looking at Mommy. The only noise in the room is the television, but no one is watching it.

"I said that sure must be a good book you're reading."

Daddy still doesn't look up, but it can't be that he doesn't hear her because she says it louder this time, louder than the television.

Carter has seen her like this before—where was it?

"Would you look at that—he's so into his book that he doesn't even notice the world around him. Doesn't even know that his wife stands before him. Is that it, is it such a good book?"

The big man isn't laughing any more. He isn't even smiling. He looks like he just said something that will get him into trouble, but he hasn't said anything.

Daddy finally glances up, again not moving his head, just lifting his eyes so that they peer over his glasses. "Yes, it is a good book."

That is all he says, and when he finishes saying it and has looked at the two of them, he lowers his eyes to his book once again and makes like he is reading, but from where he sits on the floor, Carter can see that he isn't reading because his eyes aren't moving. They are fixed on one spot, like there is a stain on the page that covers the words.

"I want you to meet Stuart," Mommy says. She says it in a friendly voice, like she is introducing an old friend, someone everyone is sure to like.

Daddy does not look up. His face shows no expression.

"Stuart, meet my husband." The big man starts to extend his hand, the hand of the arm that isn't holding Mommy—where has Carter seen her posed like that?—but then, halfway out, his hand changes its mind and slides into his pocket.

"Ted, meet Stuart."

Daddy does not look up. "I did not ask to meet him."

Stuart finally speaks. He says to Mommy, "I don't think this is a good idea."

"Don't be silly, of course it is. It's mine, isn't it?"

She laughs, but she doesn't sound happy. Carter wants to ask what is happening but somehow knows that he's not supposed to be asking questions right now. The television plays on—nobody is watching it—but it seems to play louder. The people on the television shout to be heard across the room.

Kelly shoves his yo-yo into his pocket and walks out of the chalet. Carter thinks that he's going back to the condo, but later finds he's not there. Kelly just walks out of the chalet and into the snowy winter night without a jacket or anything. Mommy doesn't seem to notice.

Mommy has that look on her face, the edges of her mouth turned down, when she can get mean, but she does not show this in the sound of her voice. Her voice still sounds polite yet shaky.

"Wouldn't you at least have the courtesy to look at him?"

"I suppose you've done enough of that for the both of us."

The big man traces his foot back and forth across the patterns of the carpet. In the lull, the television shouts from across the room.

"Come on, Beth, I think we should be going."

"No, I haven't gotten what I want."

What does she want, Carter wonders. His thoughts tangle inside. His face grows hot from questions he can't ask. Shouldn't Daddy be standing up, not shaking hands, but maybe shouting at the big man? Carter isn't sure why he thinks this, but he knows it's not right that Daddy is just sitting there with his book, not looking at either of them.

Daddy speaks again. "I never told you what to do, only asked that you not do it in front of me."

"It's been more than looking, and I've done enough of that for both of us, too."

He glares at her from over his glasses. His face looks very strained. It is the first time he looks old to Carter. "There's nothing more for me to say."

"It was good, too. Like never before."

Daddy stares back at the stain on his book, making as if to read. This isn't right. It is very, very, very wrong. But Carter still can't say what about it is wrong. The thoughts twist and twirl in his mind. He wants to scream out, to scream above the sound of the voices shouting on the television.

"Come on, Beth." Stuart tugs on Mommy's arm. "We'll go have a drink."

The picture in the living room! That's where Carter has seen her posed like that. The one where she's wearing the long white dress and Daddy's wearing the funny little black bow.

The voices on the television shriek louder. They pierce his ears. Carter can feel the blood hot in them, ready to bleed. He wants them to shut up. Shut up! SHUT UP!

"Stop it," Mommy says and yanks her arm from him. She leans over Daddy's book so that he can no longer see the stain that he is staring at. "Do you want to know how good it was?"

Carter doesn't think about it at all—it is one motion— knowing that it is as right as everything else in the room is wrong. The fire engine hurtles across the room, its white ladder spinning a half circle before it crashes into the television screen.

The shrieking stops. What follows the crash and the last crumbs of glass settling into the frame is an absolute silence, the peaceful sound of snow falling. For an instant.

Daddy leaps to his feet, shouting before he is even out of the chair, his voice harsh and violent, "What have you done?!"

Suddenly, Carter is wrapped in Mommy's arms, she kneeling beside him, and he is sobbing hard. "Get away!" She shouts at Daddy. "Get away! You've upset him enough."

Her fingers stroke Carter's hair, but he doesn't want them to. They feel like they are pressing the life out of his head, like they will crush him, that it is wrong to be touched by them. He struggles to free himself from her, but the more he struggles, the tighter she wraps her arms around him, so tight that he cannot cry out and can only feel her hands heavy upon his head.

CHAPTER 8

Saturday evening, Carter walked into the Minneapolis Athletic Club without a date. Sister Xavier had invited each of the staff to bring a guest. There were several women he could have asked, women who had served as companions at shows or parties, even hockey games; women he had never kissed good night and women with whom he had slept occasionally, but there was no special woman at the moment. No one worth pursuing. So he didn't bring a date to the fundraiser. The reason he gave himself was that he didn't want to introduce anyone to the Six West mess in the same way he wouldn't invite a date home to dinner when his family was in the midst of an argument.

Sister Xavier, clutching a nearly empty Manhattan, greeted guests at the ballroom door, beneath a hand-painted cardboard sign: *Bienvenue à Paris*. Mickey's big hand pointed to the fact that Carter was twenty minutes late, but Sister Xavier made no mention of the hour. She greeted him with a kiss on the cheek. He impulsively kissed her back, his lips landing half on her headpiece, half on her cheek, tasting both cloth and flesh. She flinched—at which he blushed and was instantly ashamed—but, then, accepting his gesture as a joke, she smiled and started to laugh.

"We've got to stop meeting like this," she said.

Carter never saw her laugh on the unit. He figured she must be feeling good because the ballroom was full. He also noticed in an offhand way, without even thinking about it, that when Sister Xavier laughed, she exposed two rows of perfect teeth.

"Carter, be a love and bring me another Manhattan." She drained her drink, catching the last ice cube in her teeth, and handed him the glass, the orange and cherry garnish still intact. "It's a cash bar, but get something for yourself, too. Tell them it's on my tab. Have anything you like—there's champagne, beer, cocktails—whatever you wish."

Carter felt like the bulimic girl whose mother offered her an extra slice of red velvet cake: *Happy Birthday!* Maybe he would have a drink—what would she say then? He headed toward the bar dragging the empty glass at his side.

Amidst the rows of dinner tables, draped with red, white, and blue tablecloths, a twenty-foot papier mâché model of the Eiffel Tower dominated the center of the ballroom. As centerpieces for each of the tables, there were flower arrangements in ceramic planter replicas of various landmarks: Notre Dame, Moulin Rouge, and Sacré-Cœur. At the end of the ballroom, behind the band, a row of cutout cardboard letters spelled the evening's theme: *Une Soirée à Paris*.

Dana leaned against the bar with Bruce. They each drank 7 Up with orange juice, Bruce's favorite drink. Dana substituted guava juice whenever he could.

"Hi, Carter. Bring your billfold?"

Bruce's humor perked him up. It usually did.

"Visa and American Express."

"Let the bidding begin!"

"When does it start?"

"After dinner," said Dana, consulting his Rolex, "which should be served in twenty-five minutes."

"Let's skip dinner and get at it," Bruce said, winking at Carter. "I'm in the mood to spend."

Dana arched an eyebrow at him. "I do hope you are joking."

He shook his head innocently. "Among these tightwads? Honey, there will be some *steals*!"

Noting Dana's reaction, Carter chipped in. "Better than bargain basement prices."

Dana spat a maraschino cherry into his glass. "You cannot be serious about supporting this fiasco."

"No, dear. I'm teasing."

"Do not do that. You had me worried. This is her worst

shenanigan yet. Absolutely shameless. And us required to subject ourselves to this...*degradation*. She has taken it too far."

Carter shifted Sister Xavier's empty glass from one hand to the other, not sure what to do with it, feeling conspicuously implicated.

"Would you look at those tacky decorations?" Dana scrunched his face. "It is all so very...*ish*. Her over there, sucking up to those overweight moneybags. Sister Mary Schmooze."

Bruce massaged the back of Dana's neck. "Now, then, it's not worth getting worked up into a lather."

"I cannot help it being here. After Thursday night. Such a disgrace. Carter, you should have seen her Thursday night." He lowered his voice to a whisper of indignation. "It was absolutely appalling."

Carter placed the glass on the bar. "Nathalie told me."

"We must do something."

"What?"

The bartender, wearing a red beret, slid down and scooped up the empty glass. "Another one?"

"Yes, a Manhattan. And coffee, black."

"Neat?"

"Huh?"

"The Manhattan—with or without ice?"

"With."

"Four-fifty."

Carter didn't think to ask if the drink would've been cheaper without ice. He had lost his sense of humor again. Instead, he looked sheepishly at Dana, but he was whispering something to Bruce. Turning from them, Carter said quickly, "Put that on Sister Mary Xavier's tab."

"Who?"

"Sister Mary Xavier," Carter hissed. "Over there."

"She your date?"

"Never mind."

Carter dug out his wallet and paid for the drinks. Thinking he might be able to slip away, he picked up the lowball tumbler and his coffee cup, leaving the saucer on the bar, but turned to find Bruce and Dana both facing him. Bruce asked, "Do we get to meet your date?"

"Didn't bring one."

Bruce pointed his eyes at the Manhattan.

"For Sister X."

Dana gave Carter an accusing look.

•••

"I just blew it with Dana."

Carter and Nathalie passed the cocktail hour on the sidelines. His coffee cup rested on the bread dish next to a miniature model of the *Arc de Triomphe* sprouting daisies.

"He sees me as an accomplice to Sister X's drinking."

Carter was angry at himself for trying to duck away.

Nathalie shook her head. Her breasts jiggled slightly—almost imperceptibly—when she did so. Distracted, Carter wondered if she was wearing a bra.

"Just one of his moods. He'll get over it."

"I couldn't have refused her."

"He'll get over it."

Nathalie looked especially pretty that evening in a black mock turtleneck and tight black stretch skirt, fishnet stockings, and black flats. She looked classy, elegant, casually refined. Even the slim crystal pendant that she wore around her neck seemed to look good, not out of place. Over the past few weeks, Carter had considered asking her out, but it would've been strange. They were pals. He could talk to her.

"No date tonight?"

"I brought Terry."

Her son. A twelve-year-old who was studious and serious. A sports nut destined to be a spectator rather than a player, the kind of kid who could quote the plus-minus ratings of the entire North Stars roster and tell you how many doubles Ted Williams hit in his rookie year, but couldn't touch a ball with a bat himself, no matter how hard he tried. Nathalie had once taken him jogging with her, but he couldn't keep up and begged to stop so he could buy baseball cards. She didn't criticize him; instead, she bought a pack herself and traded with him.

"How about you?"

"Solo again."

"What happened to what's-her-name?"

"Which one was what's-her-name?"

"The one you went away with over Valentine's. Lisa, was it?"

"Sally. I brought Lisa to the Christmas party."

"So what happened to Sally?"

"She was getting too serious. Kept talking about all her friends getting married."

"Two months ago you seemed pretty serious about her."

"That was before she started talking about marriage." Carter sipped his coffee. "I couldn't breathe."

"You're stuck in the hunt."

"I'm just looking for someone who has read Kerouac, knows the difference between icing and offsides, looks great in running shorts or an evening gown, can order for herself in a restaurant, knows how to tell a joke, and is in recovery."

"Miss Perfect."

"What's wrong with wanting someone who's got what I want?"

"If the bar is too high, you'll be looking forever. Stuck in the hunt."

Nathalie had experienced a conversion after her divorce. One day when they were having lunch at Saint Phoenix, maybe a month or two after Carter had started working at Six West, she told him the story. Her own mother had had an affair with Nathalie's husband, which had prompted the divorce, though Nathalie still loved him. Not long after, her mother died in a car accident. For a year, Nathalie told Carter, she was a mess, going to bed with any man who smiled at her and weeping herself to sleep, until one day she had a vision that changed her life. She was driving home after an exhausting day at work, in a state of despair. The night before, she had met a man who seemed nice in the grocery store but had beaten her during their lovemaking. She didn't think she could go on. She was crying and cursing at her mother when the setting sun sank beneath a low cloud and dazzled her with its brilliance. "It was no ordinary sunset—I've never seen any light that bright. The sunlight enveloped me, radiated through me, and I could feel the energy of the universe within me. I knew that if I could feel that energy at that moment when the hour was darkest for me, then that was really the truth: the light was greater than the dark; it would lead me on. A peace came over me that was so thorough that I knew if I died right then it wouldn't matter, everything would be all right. It's a wonder I didn't crash my car—I can't remember driving home."

Carter had doubted Nathalie at first—the story was so hokey. But over the months, he had watched her maintain her serenity amidst the craziness on the unit. She wasn't passive, but accepted what came her way and always came out ahead. Carter envied her that.

Mindy pranced up to the table. She sported a burgundy silk blouse, tight jeans torn à la mode at the thigh and in the rear, with black stretch pants underneath, burgundy pumps, a wristful of copper bangles, bright red nail polish, matching lipstick, and heavy green eye shadow. Her hair, swirled atop her head, tumbled about her face in a carefully styled careless look. Which way to the nightclub?

"Welcome to the lonely hearts club," Carter said.

She slid the long way around the table to sit next to him. "Hi, Carter, Nathalie."

"No date?" Nathalie asked.

"He couldn't make it."

"Someone new?"

"Relatively."

"Does feminist doctrine allow for boyfriends?" Carter asked.

She fingered the flowers in the *Arc de Triomphe*, then blurted, "He's French."

"Oh, I see. He's exempt."

"Ignore him," Nathalie said. "How'd you meet?"

"At a lecture," Mindy said, looking at Carter triumphantly. "At the Center for Women's Studies."

"A ladies' man."

She went on: He had taken her to dinner at the French consulate, treated her to fine wines, even introduced her to a count. Carter didn't believe a word of it. For starters, the nearest French consulate was in Chicago. Neither did Nathalie from the smirk he saw her trying to conceal. She excused herself to look for Terry.

"You alone tonight?" Mindy asked.

Carter pretended not to hear her. "Quite a turnout," he said, nodding toward the crowded ballroom.

"How much do you figure we'll raise?"

"What *she*'ll raise depends on the auction."

"At one hundred dollars a plate, we're not off to a bad start."

Mindy wanted to know who some of the people were. From the various boards and committees about town that Sister Xavier sat on, she had assembled quite a showing. Carter pointed out those he recognized: the publisher of the archdiocesan newspaper, a district judge, the owner of the Timberwolves, a couple of state legislators, one of the Minnesota Vikings who was there to auction a pair of season tickets, several doctors from the hospital (though only several—all were invited as Sister Mary Xavier's guests), an executive vice president from General Mills, a Danish woman who had started a popular chain of Chinese restaurants, and the owner of a very profitable office products company who had written two books about his success (the first a bestseller, the second a flop).

Mindy sipped a glass of white wine. She peered at Carter over the rim. "I'm sorry, Carter. Does it bother you if I drink?"

"Only if you get sloppy."

For all of Mindy's shortcomings, drinking wasn't one of them. She was one of those people—"normies," Carter called them, or "civilians"—who are indifferent toward alcohol. She could take it or leave it. Her type was foreign to him.

"Sister Xavier tells me you used to be quite a jock."

"Sister Xavier talks too much."

"Why don't you tell me?"

"There's not much to tell."

"She says you almost played pro hockey."

"That's an exaggeration. My mother still says the same thing. She used to tell me I had the talent to play pro. That's what she wanted more than anything, for me to play hockey."

Carter drank the final swallow of his coffee. It had gone cold.

"She used to tell me I had more talent than my brother, but he was the one to live out her dream. I became a drug counselor instead."

"Did you always want to be a drug counselor?"

"Not when I was smoking pot and getting drunk."

"I mean after. What happened?"

Carter told her about his senior year in high school. In the semifinal game of the state tournament, he had scored three goals in the first period, added another in the second, but took a penalty for interference in the third. The other team tied the game while Carter sat in the penalty box and went on to win in overtime. Afterward, the mood was glum in the dressing room. Coach Martin tried to cheer up his boys with the you-have-nothing-to-hang-your-heads-about speech, slapping Carter on the back for his four goals, but they remained mired in their mood. The team was mostly seniors that year, and many of the guys had hoped a state championship would be their ticket to play college hockey, maybe even on scholarship. They had seen people like Carter's brother Kelly accept a full ride to Harvard after his team won the state championship his senior year—Carter's freshman year—and wanted that for themselves.

While Carter walks to the shower, Mom bursts into the dressing room. The other guys scurry to cover themselves with towels. Carter has no chance; she corners him. "You owe these boys an apology."

She jabs her cigarette at him. "This game was theirs until you took a penalty in the third period of a close game."

He whiffs the cognac in her words.

"Go on, tell them you're sorry you threw away the game. Tell them you're sorry for ending their season. Tell the seniors how sorry you are their hockey careers expired in high school. Tell them you're sorry that no one remembers who finishes second. Go on, tell them."

Coach Martin tries to intervene. "Mrs. Kirchner, why don't you let the boys take their showers? You can talk to Carter at home."

She takes another step toward Carter. "Tell them you're sorry to have said you were my son, because no son of mine would have taken that penalty!"

She storms out as quickly as she came in and leaves Carter standing naked in the middle of the room. But she has broken the mood. The other guys start snapping their towels at him, jeering, "C'mon, Kirchie, say you're sorry. C'mon, one for Mommy, say you're sorry." He tries to laugh it off with them, but once in the shower her words sting like the pointed stream on his back.

He had been stoned that game. By the third period, he had crashed and wasn't high anymore, just angry. He hadn't smoked enough. If he had smoked more, he wouldn't have been so irritable, wouldn't have taken that penalty.

Carter had been high for every game that year. He led the state in scoring while stoned. Some of the games he didn't even remember. Nobody knows except a couple of teammates who smoked with him. They call Carter "Red." Coach Martin thinks it's because he lit the goal lamp so often. But it's really because of his bloodshot eyes.

At the team banquet the week following the semifinal loss,

Mom stands after the highlight film—and several drinks—to make a toast. "First, to Coach Martin: I've had two boys go through this program, watched many games and many coaches, and can honestly say, there's no finer coach in the state than Coach Martin. To you.

"Next, to the team: You boys won some close games and lost some close games, but you always played harder the next one. You played your hearts out and in the end lost a heartbreaker. When future Rochester teams look back on this season, they won't dwell on that last game. They'll remember your heart. To you.

"Finally, to my son: This year you broke all of your brother's scoring records. That should say enough. But you deserve more. I've watched you play since you used to scuff your ankles on the ice. I watched you play in the days when you skated outdoors and we kept the car running during games so you could thaw your toes between shifts. And finally these four years with the Rochester varsity. Any mother would feel blessed to have such a talented player she could call her son. I've been blessed twice with the chance to say, 'That's my boy.' Your brother is a fine hockey player, but, now, after all these years, I can finally say it, Carter: There's none finer." She holds up her cognac. "To you!"

He hates her for that. Her rage is easier to take than her praise. That night, he decides to quit hockey. He turns down all of the scholarship offers he received. No one understands. They think maybe he was burnt out on all the attention or was afraid of the expectations, but he wouldn't talk to anybody about it. Just his bong. "We bonded that winter," he said.

Mindy wiped a tear with a red fingertip.

That spring, he ends up in treatment. He turns himself in. Again, everybody is surprised. But it had gotten to the point where he wasn't getting high anymore. The pot quit working for him. He couldn't even get numb from it.

His parents want nothing to do with treatment. "You created this problem yourself—we weren't even aware of it—you must resolve it yourself," they tell him. The weekend he graduates from treatment, they fly to Boston to watch Kelly play in the Frozen Four.

His life slowly starts to take direction. He is asked to tell his story to various parent and student organizations and finds that all he lost to pot and alcohol gave him something he could share with others. He announces to his family at dinner one night that summer that he has decided to become a drug counselor. Kelly just finished his junior year at Harvard and led the Crimson in scoring. He calls Carter a wimp, accuses him of not having the balls to play with the big boys. His dad calls Carter whimsical—to his mind, an insult worse than being foolish—and has never said a word about it since. His mom starts to cry and disappears into the den. She can't separate his going through treatment with his decision not to play college hockey. She never forgives Carter for it.

Mindy looked at him with what seemed like too much sympathy. Her big green eyes shimmered with tears. He wished he hadn't talked so much about himself.

"You've been through so much."

Her voice dripped with compassion. He checked his coffee cup, but it was empty. "Not more than most people."

"Do you ever think about drinking or getting high again?"

"Sometimes. Not so much about drinking, more about getting drunk."

"Doctor Wetternach says it's progressive, that if you were to start again you would pick up where you left off. She says the urges never completely abandon the alcoholic."

"I usually go to a meeting when I get them."

"But is it hard working at Six West? I mean being around the kids—they're always talking about drugs."

"What's hard for me is hearing their problems."

"Amy Warden Schultz says the psychologist—or therapist— must find a way to detach from the patients' lives, separating her own ego from that of the patients."

"For me, it's like the story about the cop who goes out on a ledge to talk a guy out of jumping. The guy tells the cop all his reasons for wanting to jump, and the cop jumps. Sometimes I feel like the cop."

There, now he had definitely said too much. He excused himself to get another cup of coffee.

Carter found Buddha standing guard by the hors d'oeuvres table, popping Roquefort cubes into his mouth like potato chips.

"Where's Clarice?"

"Home with the bambino. Would've happily traded places, but she insisted."

Buddha's two-year-old was a cute little pudgester. His wife was as open and friendly as Buddha. They were one of the few happily married couples Carter knew.

"How's your mother?" Buddha asked.

"Sick."

"Could see that. Sorry. Know what it is?"

"Not yet. She might, but won't tell me."

"Scared?"

Carter nodded. "I wasn't until yesterday."

"Don't run from it."

"She looks worse than I've ever seen her."

"Need to talk, come to Buddha."

"Thanks."

"I mean it."

"I know."

He squeezed Carter's shoulder.

•••

Carter found his place card at a table with three hospital doctors and their wives. He knew the doctors remotely from passing them in the halls but was not on a first name basis with any. Through the courses identified on the menu card as *soupe d'oignon*; *poulet roti*, *pommes de terre rissolé*, and *haricots verts*; *salade aux tomates*; and on through the *tarte aux cerises* and *café*, he listened vaguely to the doctors' conversation about the poor upkeep of the Calhoun Beach Club's squash courts and the wives' conversation about their therapists' personality quirks. Except for the soup being too salty, the food was tasty, and the coffee, a Turkish blend, was strong, which salvaged the meal for Carter.

As refills were going around, Sister Xavier, accompanied by the band, introduced the auction. "You, the pride of this community, have further occasion this evening to arouse our pride with your generous sympathy for the young people who suffer from alcohol and drug abuse." She thrust her Manhattan over her head. "I salute each and every one of you for your continued support."

The auction opened with the smaller items—a hamper of French wines, a dozen doilies hand-crocheted in the Alsace, a set of golf clubs, Minnesota Orchestra season tickets, the Minnesota Vikings season tickets—and moved on to the grand plum: first class airfare and a week's stay for two at the

Hotel Crillon, all donations that Sister Xavier had rounded up from various local businesses. The bidding opened in friendly competition and remained generous throughout. Sister Xavier raised her glass in a toast of gratitude to each final bidder.

Carter felt conspicuous for not bidding on any item. Neither Nathalie nor Mindy bid, which offered some relief as cover, though Mindy was probably oblivious to the political implications. Howard bid early on nearly every item, though only once and each time after a nudge from Judy's elbow in his ribs. After raising his toothpick in his hand halfway, he withdrew his hand apologetically and pressed his black-rimmed glasses to the bridge of his nose.

The three doctors at Carter's table didn't bid either. "Did you see how she worked this one?"

"Benefit for the hospital, but she takes home the loot."

"Couldn't have it just for her unit because you couldn't get the write-off. Give to the hospital, and it's to a nonprofit."

Carter adopted a sudden interest in his napkin ring and sat mute.

"She fixed that with the convent?"

"Higher."

"God?"

Laughter. "No, Palmer."

"I see."

They exchanged knowing nods.

One of the wives wanted to know what her husband saw.

"She's got a keen...business sense."

"Very keen."

"Shrewd."

"Shrew?"

"Either way."

They ordered another round of drinks.

The auction ended in a rousing success, the week in Paris drawing a winning bid of $14,700. Sister Xavier, beside herself with delight, fumbled through a sloppy speech that exaggerated the virtuous improvements the money would allow Six West to make and finished with a joke. "How do you fit four alcoholics into a phone booth? Tell them there's a fifth inside."

With that, she called for the conductor to strike up the band. She initiated the dance by yanking a startled Howard from his chair and shoving him around the dance floor in a clumsy waltz. Blaming her high heels for her stumbles, she kicked them off—one landed amidst the band, only narrowly missing the bass player—and finished the waltz in her stockings.

At that, Dana and Bruce left. So did several others, including the doctor who sat to Carter's right and his wife. On his way out, Dana bent over the back of Carter's chair to whisper, "Surely you can no longer support this disgrace."

Carter felt an acute embarrassment himself, the way he did when his mom said outrageous things at holiday meals. After dinner, when off playing in the basement, he would tell his cousins that he was adopted and secretly wish he could make it true by saying so.

Nathalie filled the seat beside him vacated by the doctor. He wanted to ask her to dance, which ordinarily would have been no problem. They'd had fun dancing at the Christmas party and on other occasions. The problem was that he had started thinking of asking her to dance the way he would ask a date. He found himself rehearsing the line in his head: *Shall we dance?* Or maybe a little more suggestively, *Let's dance.* Which made him hesitate.

Her foot kept time, swinging, one-two-three, one-two-three. Her shoes—flats, not heels—could not be an excuse. He finally leaned forward; she turned to him. They both opened their mouths, about to speak, but seeing the other, paused. Go ahead, Carter nodded. She placed her hand casually on his knee, "You're chewing your tongue."

Carter felt his cheeks flame. "I didn't realize it."

"I'm going to take Terry for a whirl."

"Oh."

"There you go again."

"What?"

"Chewing your tongue."

He caught himself as soon as she said it. "Bad habit."

"It's kind of cute. What were you going to say?"

"Nothing."

As she led her son through the cluster of tables to the dance floor, his eyes followed her wistfully. The scent of her perfume lingered.

Just then, Mindy appeared at his side. She had a knack for inopportune timing. Her hand on his right shoulder, she leaned over to whisper in his left ear, "Will you dance with me?"

The way that she bent at the waist afforded a clear view of her swaying breasts, round and a little chubby but with generous brown nipples. No question whether or not *she* wore a bra. The mood had deserted Carter.

"No, thanks. I don't dance."

"But Carter," she said, and swiveled a little to grant him a better view, enhanced by the sway of motion. "You said yesterday how much you love to waltz."

He glanced from her breasts to the dance floor where Nathalie eased her son tenderly through the steps then back up to Mindy's lusty yet uncertain eyes. "No, I don't dance."

When Nathalie returned to the table, innocently pleased by her dance with her son, they slid easily back into their earlier conversation, joking about the band members' haircuts, tacitly ignoring Sister Xavier's drunken court at the head table, and confiding that they had wanted to bid on several items but hadn't for fear of Dana's wrath. The moment of question, when the future of their relationship hung suspended in uncertainty, had passed. To Nathalie, unwittingly. To Carter, all too familiarly.

CHAPTER 9

————

Carter had just consulted Mickey when Mindy rushed up to the table. Mickey stopped traffic except for cars turning right: quarter to midnight. The crowd had thinned some, but the band played on and the dance floor was still swinging. Mindy bent to whisper in Nathalie's ear but had to straighten herself, hand to her chest, before she could speak. She tried again in a ferocious whisper. Her hand flapped to animate her words. Nathalie's expression changed from agitation to alarm.

"You're sure?"

Mindy nodded, breathless from the rush of words. Nathalie hopped up and wove her way through the dinner tables out of the ballroom and down the hall. Mindy and Carter hustled to keep up with her.

Without breaking stride, they marched into the tiny women's restroom at the end of the hallway, a windowless cell ignored during the athletic club's recent renovations. The original brown brick, dating back to the turn of the century, crumbled from the upper corners. They tumbled upon Judy, who stood alone in front of the solitary wooden stall, its door closed, waiting her turn politely though somewhat impatiently, clearing her throat and tapping her foot. The trio's sudden entry startled her. She fixed her dumbfounded stare on Carter.

Mindy pointed to the closed stall. "In there."

"Excuse me," Judy said. "Would it be too much to ask what's going on?"

Nathalie's eyes tentatively followed the trail from Mindy's extended arm to the stall door, shedding white paint like old skin.

Judy, not waiting for an explanation, turned to where Nathalie's eyes paused, and knocked. The door swung open slowly, its widening arc gradually revealing the stall's occupant.

Her legs were spread askew as though they had fallen carelessly from her body when it collapsed astride the toilet. Her hands hung limply and heavily at her sides against the porcelain. Her bare head slouched back against the wall at an awkward angle that one would not tolerate in normal sleep. Her face gleamed pale against the brick, the eyes not completely closed, showing thin egg-white slits to the four staff members gaping at her. Her mouth hung slack. A strand of vomit dangled from her lower lip like a thread of mozzarella cheese.

"Sister Mary Xavier!" Judy gasped.

Mindy leaned against the brick wall, stunned.

Carter could not bring himself to look at Sister Xavier's prone figure slumped on the toilet. His gaze deferred to her fallen headpiece crumpled at her feet. *Damn.*

"Looks like a Maalox moment," Nathalie quipped.

Judy's first instinct was as a nurse. She moved forward to check the pulse at the neck, her watch already raised as her fingers made contact with the pale flesh.

Satisfied with the pulse, she said to no one in particular, "Help me lay her on the floor."

Mindy and Carter squeezed into the narrow stall with Judy, but none of them could position themselves to bend over to grip the body. Searching for an angle to get a hold with some leverage, Carter gagged on the stench of humid puke. The thought of hoisting Sister Xavier's limp body like a sack of mail or a bulky mattress mortified him.

"We can't leave her in here," Nathalie said. "We've got to take her somewhere more discreet."

Judy glowered at Nathalie, her beady eyes nearly bursting out of her skull. She was the nurse. "First things first. She's unconscious."

"We need smelling salts," Mindy exclaimed suddenly, as though remembering the answer to an exam question.

"Oh, of course. Right there next to the soap dispenser."

"Shut up, Carter." She appealed to Nathalie. "I mean that

we could get some."

"Where?"

"I don't know." That part hadn't been on the test. "The kitchen?"

"How are you going to explain that?" Carter asked. "Excuse me, Sister X is passed out in the bathroom, mind if I borrow your smelling salts?"

"I wouldn't ask like *that*."

"You know, I don't think it's the best idea to revive her," Nathalie said. "It might be easier to move her while she's unconscious."

"To carry her?" Mindy asked, unwilling to admit defeat.

"If conscious, she could resist."

"She should not be moved," Judy insisted. "She should be laid out with her feet elevated and her head turned to the side, in case she vomits again."

They remained cramped in the tiny stall, Nathalie at the door, standing between Sister X's sprawled feet, as though in a crowded elevator. One of Mindy's hands rested absentmindedly on Sister X's shoulder. Sister X slumbered in the heart of them, unconscious, her immediate presence nearly forgotten, though her condition foremost in their minds. Carter shifted his weight and leaned against the tampon receptacle on the wall, then, suddenly realizing what it was, jerked his arm away.

"We could disguise her," Mindy suggested.

They all looked at her—*What?*

"Carry her out as one of us...swap clothes...or..." The idea quickly lost steam under their collective look. "Or...pretend that...forget it."

Carter believed something definitely needed to be done, but he was at a loss himself for what that something was.

"If we believe the Al-Anon philosophy we preach to parents, why should we rescue her?" Nathalie said. "Why not leave her where she is—let her suffer whatever natural consequences follow?"

"What if that reporter finds her?" Mindy asked.

"We've got to get her out of here," Carter said.

"She can't be moved."

"Judy, we can lay her out somewhere else," Carter said. "Sit with her until she comes to, but this isn't the place. Someone could walk in at any moment."

"Someone's got to guard the door," Mindy said.

They turned to Carter. "What do I say?" he asked weakly.

"Tell them the toilet is clogged," Nathalie said. "Ask them to use another."

They shifted and shuffled in the tight space so Carter could squeeze past them. On his way out, between the two sets of doors, he ran into one of the doctor's wives. Startled, she glanced from Carter to the sign on the outer door and back to him.

"I'm sorry," he said. "This one is full."

He chewed his tongue nervously. She stared incredulously at him.

"I just checked. On my date." Then he remembered that she had sat at his table. "I mean, my friend. A friend. She tells me it's full. Uh, could you please use another?"

"Which—the men's?"

"No, no...no. There's another, I'm sure, uh, downstairs in the lobby. Yes, please try the lobby."

The woman eyed Carter strangely, as though she had caught him peering under the stalls. She turned and walked down the hall, shaking her head.

Carter felt his knees quaking. He had nearly blown it.

Standing guard outside of the door, feeling conspicuously removed from the situation, hearing their hollow voices from within, the debate on what course of action to take echoing off the brick walls, he remembered the scene in *The Bonfire of the Vanities* where the mistress's wealthy husband dies in a Chinese restaurant and they pass him out the bathroom window feet first. When he read that passage, Carter had laughed aloud; standing outside the bathroom, it now seemed a brainstorm. They could pass Sister X out the window, have a car waiting outside, and drive her back to the convent. She would be safe, no one would notice. *That was it!* He had found the solution.

When Carter burst back into the bathroom, the three women still bickered over the prone figure. They all jumped at his sudden entry.

"I've got it," he said, but immediately realized his mistake. The tiny bathroom had no window.

"What?"

"What is it?"

They looked at him, expectant, wanting to be relieved. He had also forgotten that they were on the second floor.

"Never mind."

He exited as abruptly as he had entered, feeling a slow impotent anger smoldering in his chest. His eyes burned a hole in the carpet where he fixed them. The voices from within resumed their debate.

Howard walked timidly around the corner, one hand in his pocket, the other reaching up to poke his glasses into place. He stepped cautiously, self-consciously, as though not wanting to make any noise on the carpeted hallway. Carter had never liked Howard. He was a man subordinate to his wife with no guts or volition of his own. When Judy bullied him in public, he joked in his defense, pushing up his glasses, that he always got the last word, "Yes, dear."

"Say, Carter, have you seen my wife? You must be waiting for your date yourself. We men spend half our lives waiting for women, heh, heh."

At that moment, in the way the light caught Howard's glasses, Carter saw a double image: both his father's reflection against the lenses and Howard's magnified anxious eyes behind them. Carter recognized that he was chewing his tongue.

A commotion sounded from the bathroom. Scattered clicking of heels on the tiles, the thumping stumbling of bodies. Suddenly forgetting himself, Carter checked the hallway to see that the coast was clear, even peered down the stairway. He turned and was nearly run over by Sister Xavier herself. She bumped full against his chest, stumbled back two steps, and stared blankly into his face. They stood frozen for a moment, long enough for him to note the slimy smear on her chin, the wild vacant look in her eyes. Then she strode off, taking deliberate steps like a drunk speaking slowly, pronouncing each step carefully. Headpiece crumpled in one hand, she clasped the rail with the other and stomped down the stairs without missing a step.

Mindy, Nathalie, and Judy spilled out of the bathroom after her. Howard, who had backpedaled half a dozen steps to let Sister X pass, nearly losing his balance with his hands still in his pockets, looked completely baffled by the outpouring of women from the rest room.

"Which way did she go?" Mindy asked.

Howard, pressing up his glasses with his ring finger and

chuckling again to himself, said, "I'll never understand this need women have to go to the bathroom in groups."

CHAPTER 10

———

Sunday morning, Carter awoke with an emotional hangover. There was a time—after he had started smoking pot and drinking—when he awoke without feeling. He could convince himself the night or day before hadn't happened, simply dissolve it in his memory. Treatment had spoiled that skill. The bruised feeling of the morning after assured him they had found Sister X passed out in the toilet. He felt sluggish, like he had slept too much, though the shadows across his bedroom told him it must be only around 8:30.

The sky outside his window was a gray-white glare. Lifting his head from the pillow, he could see that the snow had started again: large, white, thick flakes coated the once bare branches of the elm that brushed his window. The shadows from the branches formed bars on the wall next to his bed.

He's twelve, his brother fifteen, on a hot summer day. They have been fishing, just the two of them, and return home before lunch. The morning sun is already too hot for the fishing to be good anymore, not that it has been great that morning, though they had enough bites to make them quarrel about who will carry the stringer home. Kelly, being bigger, wins the argument, and Carter lugs the fish over his handlebars up the hill.

Usually Brandy runs to greet them. They have taken her fishing in the past, but she's a chocolate lab and gets too excited. When they have a fish nearly reeled into shore, she jumps into the water and attacks the line. Carter would have brought her anyway to play with during the lulls between bites, but since she is Kelly's dog, a special present on his tenth birthday—"the best birthday ever"—Brandy stayed home.

This morning Brandy does not rush out to greet them when they pedal up the hill. She does not nose about when they park their bicycles in the garage and Carter plops the stringer of fish in the outside sink. She does not bark when they walk inside.

Mom sits at the kitchen table, silently smoking a cigarette. She somberly watches the boys take off their muddy shoes at the back door, does not respond to their greeting, but follows them with her heavy-lidded look across the room.

"Brandy!" Kelly calls.

The house is so still you can hear the tobacco hiss when Mom drags on her cigarette.

"Brandy! Here, girl."

Mom looks out the window. She addresses the trees outside the window, stiffly, like one of them. "Brandy is dead."

"What?"

Kelly stands over her, twice as tall as she in the chair. She looks at him as though seeing him for the first time. "She was sleeping under the car. I didn't see her."

She laughs—a hysterical pitch that shrieks in their ears. The laugh gains force until the tears come, and she explodes into heavy sobs.

Kelly loses it. He flails at her with open palms. She raises her hands, clutches her head, and continues to sob. He strikes her about the shoulders and arms and hands and head, not looking where he strikes but flailing with an unseeing force. He screams above her sobs, "You killed my dog! You killed my dog!" Over and over, striking at her with his open palms.

Carter stands by, watching helplessly. He knows that he should stop his brother, but he makes no movement toward him. She should not have killed his dog. She should not have been drinking. Maybe she only started drinking afterward. Maybe not. It was always hard to tell which came first. Carter does not stop his brother, and he does not leave. He stands and watches him flail at her.

Before dinner, just before the time that Dad arrives home, she comes into his room and makes him sit next to her on the bed. Her face is decorated with different colors of makeup, but the colors cannot hide her swollen and puffed eye. She does not smell like she's been drinking.

"Carter," she says.

He looks away to the window.

"Carter." She turns his chin to her with her eyes.

"Brandy was hit by a car, and Mommy bumped into a door. Do you understand?"

She told him such stories when he was younger; he has come to accept them on faith like fairy tales. But it was easier when he was younger.

He stares outside at the trees. Something in him hardens like their bark. He does not answer her.

"Carter, be a good boy. Brandy was hit by a car, and Mommy bumped into a door. Okay?"

He nods without looking at her. When she leaves, he unpacks his bong from where he keeps it hidden deep inside his bag of hockey equipment.

Dad had not asked about the dog during dinner but did later when the house seemed especially calm. Mom told him Brandy had been hit by a car. Hit and run. Carter doesn't know if he asked about her eye. As far as he knows, Dad still believes that Brandy had been the victim of a hit and run and that Mom's eye had been an accident.

CHAPTER 11

"Cirrhosis?"

"That's what the tests show," Dad said.

Despite what Carter knew, he clung to the notion that cirrhosis was something that happened only to winos on the street. He had prepared himself for cancer. That he could accept. But cirrhosis? That was synonymous with skid row. Yet that's what Dad had told him: she had cirrhosis.

She slept—or was anesthetized, he could not tell. She had been unconscious when Carter had arrived at her room. She looked worse than when he had seen her Friday. Her face was bruised and swollen, with a pastiness about the eyes. Little red marks spidered her bare, pale arms. A drip IV tube, attached to her left arm, handcuffed her to the machine at her side. Covered only by a flimsy hospital gown, she looked terribly out of place propped in that bed on the second floor of Saint Jude's. The sight of her sickness stirred in his throat. Carter tasted the acid burn the back of his mouth. He meant to kiss her but couldn't bring himself to do it. She looked as he imagined a leper would.

He had arrived late. His car had stalled a couple of times along the way. He was supposed to have met Kelly and Dad at noon. Kelly had been there since Saturday evening.

"How accurate are the tests?" Kelly cross-examined Dad. He wore a gray double-breasted suit and a striped tie, which made Carter conscious of his own jeans and sneakers.

"Jenkins is tops in his field."

"How bad is it?"

"Yesterday's biopsy confirmed that she has portal cirrhosis. The chemical tests confirmed the presence of increased bilirubin, a bile pigment in the blood that has produced early stages of jaundice."

"What's the treatment?"

"Jenkins has her started on diuretics, which is to counteract the edema, or excessive accumulation of water fluid in body cavities. We've discussed cortisone but haven't reached agreement on its administration. In the meantime, complete bed rest, dietary and vitamin supplements, and abstinence."

"It will take three days for her to detox," Carter said. "Will she be able to get through that?"

"I haven't discussed that with Jenkins."

Kelly pushed back his stiff cuff with a forefinger. "I've got a 3:15 flight. Either of you going by the airport?"

It was as though they were oblivious to his mother lying between them: Dad sounding like a textbook, Kelly preoccupied by his flight.

Carter had tried to talk to Kelly about her several years ago. The two of them had been fishing in Canada. Kelly took an annual trip there on Labor Day, but that year his college buddies had all been busy. Carter had agreed to go, thinking it might be a chance to regain some of the ground that had come between them since Kelly had left for Harvard.

Carter broaches the subject on their drive north. "You know what she said to me last night?"

"Mom?"

"She said, 'I should've been a nun after all.'"

"She in one of her religious moods?"

"I was telling her about one of the kids I work with."

"She never says that kind of thing to me unless she's in one of her religious moods."

"She never said that before to me."

"You've got to understand," he says, looking at Carter with one eye. "She doesn't think when she says these things. She's just being emotional."

"She'd been drinking. That's what it was."

"You make too much of that."

"Kelly, she's always drinking. Ever since we were kids."

"You've got to remember, not everyone's an alcoholic. Just

because you might be or the kids you work with are, doesn't mean everyone is."

"It's not that I might be. I am."

"Whatever, she's not."

"Don't you remember finding cognac bottles all over the house, even in the skate box? How we couldn't bring friends home from school because we didn't know if she'd be passed out? How Dad made Spam sandwiches for dinner?"

Kelly stares at the road ahead of him. "I don't think about it. I'm not sure I'd remember if I did."

"What about Brandy? She was drunk then."

"That's past," he snaps. "Leave it alone."

They drive several miles without speaking. Kelly grips the wheel rigidly. Carter watches the pines and birches slip past his window.

"You've got to get on with your life, that's all," Kelly says suddenly.

More miles and trees slip by.

"I did," he says.

"And I didn't?"

"You ever going to college?"

"It's too late to play hockey."

"For an education."

"I don't see why. I like what I'm doing."

"That hurt her. When you didn't go. She thought you did

it to spite her. Maybe that's why she says those things."

"She says those things only when she's been drinking."

It ended like that, each of them convinced the other was wrong. They spent the rest of the weekend talking sports. Kelly finished off a case of beer, and Carter did not bring up the family again.

It was the same with Dad. Only a couple of weeks after Carter had completed treatment, Mom had been pulled over for swerving down South Broadway. The policeman was going to charge her with DWI until he realized who she was. He apologized, but she complained about him terribly that night at dinner.

Later, Carter asks his dad, "Don't you think she drinks too much?"

"She's had a hard life, Son."

"But she's always drinking."

"I've never yelled at your mother, not even raised my voice. I've tried to be sympathetic."

"But, Dad—"

"She bears up quite well, I think, all things considered."

Carter knows in his gut that Dad is wrong, but he is unable to reason with him.

Her broken figure in the hospital bed accused Carter of his own guilt. He too willfully pushed aside her alcoholism, was not willing to confront it by himself. He needed someone to verify it for him. Denied that, he was paralyzed on his own. So he distanced himself from his mother, trying to believe that what he didn't see she didn't suffer. Yet the knowledge of what he was doing nagged at him—his own treatment had spoiled the comforts of denial. As a result, he had thrown himself deeper into his work.

Carter felt the fury swelling within his chest. "You should've done something sooner."

"It's a little late to start throwing around blame," Kelly said. He fiddled with his cuff. "Dad, you have time to give me a lift?"

"That cough must have worried you."

"Bronchitis. She smokes a pack a day. Even now, she refuses to quit."

"What about her coloring—couldn't you see it changing?"

"Shit, Carter," Kelly said. "She goes to a tanning booth twice a week. Lay off."

"Dad, her stomach's swollen, for Christ's sake."

"You know no one can say anything to her about her weight."

Carter wanted to see some emotion in him, some spark of life. But instead he stood there calm and bland. "Dad, you watched her drink for twenty-five years and did nothing. Now it's come to this."

"Cirrhosis has various causes, son."

"DAD! She's an alcoholic. She'll die if she doesn't quit."

"Listen, hotshot," Kelly said. "It's not his fault."

The way he leaned across the bed, Carter thought his brother might hit him. "If you're the expert, why didn't you do something sooner?"

"I tried. You told me to go to college."

"It won't help her now for you to chastise others."

"She must stop drinking."

"Let the doctors take care of her. You don't need to make her—or us—feel any worse."

He left to call a taxi.

Dad fidgeted across the bed. "Let's talk about you getting a new car, Son. I'll cosign for you, if that's what's holding you up."

Carter saw his father again as old—the age spots on his forehead, the thin strands of hair at his temples, the weak look in his eyes. He, along with Kelly, had resigned himself to defeat. Next to his wife, he stood frail and helpless. He could do nothing for her.

Carter wanted to crush his jaw with his fist.

CHAPTER 12

By Monday morning the snow had stopped. Sunday's outburst had dumped nearly a foot of white, thick powder across the city. In the street, the snow had buried Carter's car, along with all of the others parked outside. The white even mounds that lined one side of the street looked like a row of freshly filled graves. Climbing inside the car, quiet and dark—the windshield blocked by the layer of snow—was like entering a tomb. An eerie stillness filled the interior. His routine was to start the car, then clear the windows while the engine warmed up. That morning, the Prelude didn't start. The eerie stillness extended to its engine.

Carter called the garage as Nathalie told him he should've done earlier. Then he called her for a ride, but she had already left. There was a forty-five minute wait for a taxi, so he gave in to the bus, which took almost as long as the taxi by the time he had trudged through the snow to the bus stop, waited, transferred downtown, and walked the last two blocks to the hospital. Throughout, he continued to consult Mickey, watching his hand swing round like a softball pitcher's, and delivered a long monologue to himself that detailed the inefficiencies of the Minneapolis public transit system. By the time he traipsed into the hospital a half hour late, he had firmly resolved to find a ride home rather than take the bus again.

In the lobby, while he stomped the snow off his sneakers and finished cursing public transit, he noticed a young guy, college age, with bangs clipped unevenly across his forehead, a beak nose and gap tooth, who looked like he could be David Letterman's little brother. The guy carried a large philodendron. Carter watched him approach an elderly woman who peered at the gift shop window display. "Excuse me, ma'am. I'm sorry to trouble you, really, but I was wondering if you might bring this plant to my mother. See, she's very sick, and it hurts me too much to see her that way. Would you be so kind as to do me this favor? It would mean so much."

The elderly woman accepted the plant with an expression of deep sympathy. Overhearing him, Carter saw his own mother's face in his mind's eye—the jaundiced and bruised portrait against the hospital pillow. The young guy gave the elderly woman the room number, thanked her profusely, and left.

•••

Upstairs, Nathalie beckoned Carter into her office. Dana posed next to the file cabinet, one hand in his pocket. Nathalie's office was a twin of Carter's—same size, same furniture—but hardly identical. Nathalie had fitted the windows with lace curtains and replaced the overhead fluorescent light with a beaded-shade floor lamp. Dangling against the window, from a strand of fishing line, was a crystal pendant that spotted the walls with prisms of light. A collection of shells and agates spread over the top of her olive-drab file cabinet, with conch shells clustered on the floor. A small tape deck atop the cabinet played a recording of flute solos from the base of the Grand Canyon. Dana punched the stop button with his forefinger.

"I am sorry, but I cannot stand any more of that nonsense." For Dana, if it wasn't opera, it wasn't music. "What this New Age calls music is no more than a mellifluous mess."

"We were discussing Sister X," Nathalie said to Carter.

He helped himself to a cup of coffee. "I can't think of a better way to start the day."

Dana scowled at him. He proposed that they request a headquarters consultant visit the unit, say to advise them on the implementation of the new client privacy regulations. Once the consultant had arrived, the three of them—and Mindy, if she would cooperate, since she was also a witness Saturday night—would meet with the consultant alone to present the case against Sister Xavier.

In the early days, two decades before treatment became big business of the eighties and recovery from chemical dependency simply another commodity on the market, Saint Jude's had pioneered a new approach to treating alcoholics. Carter had heard the stories passed on by Nathalie and Buddha and others who had worked with some of the old-timers. Six West had been a free-wheeling place, full of energy and innovation, run by the counselors, many of them recovering alcoholics and addicts themselves. They struck upon the Minnesota Model, a marriage of the Twelve Steps with psychotherapy, what came to serve as the paradigm for treatment centers worldwide. A decade later, when Six West expanded its recovery program to treat drug abuse as well, it coined the term chemical dependency. Thus, Saint Jude's, an unassuming brick structure across the Mississippi River from the University of Minnesota, became known throughout the country, indeed throughout the world, as the patriarch of treatment centers. Saint Jude's was to chemical dependency what the Mayo Clinic was to medicine. Together, they put Minnesota on the world health care map.

But, during the last few years, when Six West struggled to maintain the eighties' brisk economic pace—the proliferation of treatment centers as rapid and widespread as a teenager's acne—and prided itself too much on its past, thinking reputation was enough to beat the competition and defend itself against the inquisitions of frugal insurance companies, the suits came in. Two years ago, the Sisters of Humility, stewards of the hospital, sold off Six West to CareCorps, Inc., manager of two hundred treatment centers nationwide, all operated under the same ideology, regardless of race, religion, or location. The nuns still ran the hospital, and they had insisted that one of their own be the first executive director. Sister Mary Xavier, being the first and only nun of the order to hold an MBA, and having proven her skill by putting the nursing home's finances back into the black, was the nuns' natural choice. But, even with a nun at its helm— or, some might say, especially with Sister X in charge—Six West now belonged to the treatment industry. Quotas, cost-effectiveness, and quality service had slipped into Six West's jargon. Headquarters had closed the adult unit after only six months and put its money behind the adolescent unit. No longer distinguished along the cutting edge of health care, Six West had become simply another business; it had faded into the obscurity of any other franchise: McTreatment.

On the employee bulletin board, someone—probably Dana—had altered the CareCorps tagline from "We care about people" to "We care about profits." It was true. The greed of free enterprise had perverted treatment. The suits' primary purpose was not to help the addict who still suffered—it was to profit from him. The insurance companies tried to check this expansion of exploitation—not out of any goodness in their heart, but out of the reverse greed: to cut down costs. To Carter's way of thinking, they had swung too far to the other extreme of denying treatment at the expense of the addict.

Carter defended treatment on two counts. First, the setting was likely to break through the armor of the alcoholic's denial sooner than a simple A.A. meeting. Second, all of the information and support jump-started one's sobriety. He didn't deny that for some A.A. was enough, but treatment had worked for him, and he believed it was invaluable to others as well. Like Dana, though perhaps for different reasons, he wanted Six West to survive.

"You want to bring in one of the suits?" Carter challenged Dana. "They know less about chemical dependency than she does—how do you expect them to understand the problem?"

"We will hit them where they do understand—in the bottom line. Our case will be this: Sister Xavier's drinking has been bad for business."

"Won't it be hard to convince them of that after Saturday night? I heard she raised eighty grand."

"Judy told me the same. It will be long-term versus short. They will have to weigh the risks of her reputation destroying theirs."

"But why one of the suits?"

"Because she is the convent's pet. They would not consider removing her."

"Even if they knew of the boozing and carousing?"

"Never underestimate a nun's power of denial."

"Good point."

"So far as the hospital brass goes, if she is protecting Palmer, he probably has some reason to protect her. It would be too much of a risk to approach him."

"That leaves headquarters," Nathalie said.

"What about Judy? Wouldn't it be best to have a united front?"

"She's not a Six West employee," Dana said.

"But Howard is. She could use him to sabotage our plan."

"If we have adequate documentation, plus Mindy," Nathalie said, "we should be able to make a strong enough case."

"Still, Judy worries me. She could report us to Sister X, and we'd all be out looking for work this afternoon."

"It is a risk," Dana acknowledged. "But one we must take."

Buddha knocked. "Hiding out?"

"We were discussing what to do about Saturday night." Dana summarized his plan.

"'Bout time," Buddha said. "She needs help."

Carter still wasn't sold on the plan. He knew something needed to be done, that the problem had to be addressed, but he wasn't sure that this was the right way. When you got right down to it, you had to choose the good of the kids over Sister Xavier's fate, yet he felt a loyalty to her for the confidence she had placed in him. Suspicious of Dana's motives, he wanted to protect Sister X.

Dana interpreted Carter's brooding as consent. "One of us will have to call headquarters to request the consultant. As you know, I am not technically a CareCorps employee; like Judy, my contract is with the hospital. Nevertheless, any one of you could make the call."

Nathalie offered. "I have a friend at HQ who might be able to set something up for us."

"Remember, it must look like he initiated the visit," Dana continued. "He cannot let on that we called him in."

"I'll take care of it."

CHAPTER 13

The weekend, as usual, had been eventful for the kids. Whitney sported a new hickey—she told Judy that she burned herself with her curling iron. Judy was not amused. Whitney wouldn't name the guy who had given it to her, and none of the guys came forward to admit it. Frustrated that she could not give Whitney a consequence on the level board, Judy gave her a lecture instead.

The other kids had put Archie up to a prank that backfired. He smeared shaving cream on the earpiece of the telephone at the nurses' station then called Mindy, who had stopped in on Sunday, to the phone. She had taken it personally, even after he apologized, and gave him a day drop on the level board for using the phone without staff permission.

Rodney had solemnly and straightforwardly turned in Chip for smoking in the bathroom, as though reluctant to tell on Chip, but seeing it as his only recourse. Chip received a day drop for contraband.

The weekend night nurse had found Oscar sitting in his window after lights out listening to Rodney's Walkman. When she told Oscar he had to turn it off and get into bed even if he couldn't sleep, he growled in such a fierce whisper, "Fuck off," that she backed out of the room and refused to check on him the rest of the evening.

His urinalysis came back from the lab clean, as Carter had suspected it would. Carter finally got through to Oscar's mother on one of her breaks at the plastics-molding plant. She had nothing to offer. She had shut down herself. First her husband had left her for booze, then her son for drugs. She had no faith in treatment centers and, telling Carter she would get into trouble for talking past the end of her break, hung up.

Oscar's probation officer, a grizzled ex-con from the same school as Officer Patterson, was also no help. He could not understand why the judge had sent Oscar to treatment. "Why coddle these kids? Won't do any good. They'll never learn if they don't feel their own pain."

That morning, when Carter sat down with Oscar to complete his psycho/social history, Oscar maintained his reticent defiance. This time, no amount of prodding, joking, or cajoling would budge him. He stared Carter down with granite eyes. Cold. Impenetrable. *You want me to tell you my life story so you can write it all down in your notes? Fuck off.*

So much for Carter's weekend adjustment strategy.

"You told me about the last night you got drunk, I'll tell you about mine. When the cops broke up the party, they hauled me and a few others who were shit-faced into the station. I refused to tell them my name. I was so drunk I figured that if they didn't know who I was, I couldn't get into trouble."

Oscar stared him down.

"Later I learned that they let the other kids call their parents to come pick them up. They threw me into detox. I still refused to tell them my name, so they stuffed me into a tiny isolation cell. I thought they would tire of me, let me go, and I would hitchhike home. I wasn't sure where I was, but whoever picked me up would know how to get to Pill Hill—where the doctors lived. I would sneak into the house, and my parents would never have to know what happened."

Oscar stared without expression, but Carter sensed he hadn't lost him.

"Overhead there was this awful fluorescent light that was giving me a headache, it was so bright. I lay on a thin mattress in the tiny cell but kept one foot on the concrete floor to keep the room from spinning. Every so often they checked on me through the window of the locked door. I could not turn off the light from the inside."

He paused. Oscar, almost in spite of himself, said, "And?"

"I puked."

Oscar snorted a short, sharp laugh.

"I frantically scooped my puke under the mattress trying to hide the fact I was drunk."

Oscar shook his head.

"They kept me there for three days. In my more sober moments, I was able to see the gap between the way I thought things were and the way they really were. That was the beginning of my recovery."

"Did you tell them your name?"

"When I sobered up."

"I wouldn't have done that."

"Why not?"

He wouldn't say. They engaged in another silent duel.

But not for long. Nathalie knocked on the door—time for group. Rodney was scheduled to present his Fifth Step.

CHAPTER 14

Rodney sat erect in his chair, the fringes of his brown suede jacket hanging still. His solemn bearing quieted the other kids.

"There weren't any tunnels or bright lights—all I remember is darkness: a thick, heavy blackness surrounded me. Like I was drowning in melted tar. It choked my lungs and filled my eyes. I was sinking into the blackness but couldn't do anything to stop it, just felt this heavy weight absorb my body. That was the first time.

"The nurse told me later that she thought I was a goner. She couldn't find a pulse. Couldn't hear a heartbeat. Nothing. Nothing on the monitors, either. The doctors told me, too. They thought I was a goner. They all carried on about it, me lying in the bed, and them talking about blood alcohol level and me flatlining and shaking their heads.

"The whole time they're talking to me I kept seeing that blackness in my eyes and I started rubbing to make it go away, and suddenly the nurse is asking what's wrong and I'm telling them I've got tar in my eye and they finally look at me instead of talking about their monitors and tell me I need to rest. But I kept rubbing at my eyes until they started to bleed, trying to rub the blackness away and burping blackberry brandy.

"This Dakota dude I had seen at the pool hall but didn't know his name, a big guy already sixteen, not so much blubber as just big: wrists thick as my calves, legs like my waist, and lump of a head the size of a rock you couldn't lift; this guy who's got a reputation for being able to outdrink anyone, walked into the back of Walgreens where Janine works during the day but at night we were smoking cigarettes and the others were huffing fingernail polish. This dude, who knows a cousin of Janine's, walked into the back of the store with his case of blackberry brandy and challenged anyone to a duel.

"No one would take him on, they were scared by his reputation, so I did, out of curiosity, I guess, because I wanted to see if it was true about how much he could drink, but also because I didn't like huffing. It just gives—or, gave—me a headache. I wanted to get drunk."

Chip and Archie nodded. Made sense to them.

"Janine—that's my girlfriend—was saying, 'No, Rodney. Don't, Rodney,' but I had made up my mind, and she couldn't stop me. We sat on stacks of magazines across from one another, each with our own bottle, and matched shots. He didn't even grimace when he drank. Just stuck the bottle to his big lips and the brandy disappeared. After four or five shots apiece, Janine started pleading with me again, tugging on my arm, 'Rodney, please, don't. Let's go. Please, let's leave.' But the fuel had started to work. I wasn't going anywhere. She kept tugging on my arm, 'Rodney, please, I want to go, please, Rodney.' When she wouldn't shut up—'Rodney, please!'—I slapped her."

He paused. Lowered his voice.

"I slapped her.

"I had never slapped her before. Afterward she looked at me with saucer eyes and tears covered them up and spilled down her cheeks. 'You wanna leave? Then leave!' I shouted at her. She did."

His usually stoic voice leaked emotion. The rest of the kids listened raptly.

"I went back to taking shots, it was my turn. I lost track at fifteen, but I remember fifteen because at fifteen I thought to myself, 'Now I've taken one for each birthday.'

"After I got out of the hospital, my friends wanted to celebrate. They said I'd done twenty-two shots and that the big Dakota dude had passed out at twenty. I don't remember the ambulance or any of that, don't even know if they were right, but they kept saying I'd done twenty-two shots and that was a record.

"Janine made me promise I would never drink again, so

I had to sneak it from her. When she caught me drinking, it was the same thing: she bitched at me and something came over me that I couldn't stop—it never happened when I wasn't drinking—and I slapped her until she shut up. After awhile, I had to slap her more to get her to shut up."

Rodney paused. He had never told anyone this. He studied his hands. He did not seem to recognize them as part of himself. He raised them in front of him and cried out, "What have you done?"

Again, he cried, "What have you done?!"

He began to beat his hands against his thighs. He slapped them hard, like swinging a fish's head against a rock to knock it unconscious. His hands slapped with growing intensity—whack, whack! WHACK! The rest of the group sat stunned and hushed.

Oscar reached out and grabbed his roommate's wrists. He pressed them against his thighs. After holding them there a moment, he placed one arm around Rodney's shoulder, not speaking, just holding him.

Rodney melted into Oscar, his weight sinking into Oscar's chest, and he began to sob.

"I...wish...that...was...someone...else," he gasped between sobs.

Oscar cradled Rodney under his arm, rocked him back and forth, still not saying anything.

"I...hurt...her...bad."

He sobbed in deep gushes. Oscar rocked him.

Then, something in Rodney strengthened, like coil straightening itself. "I don't want to hurt her or me or anybody. No more."

CHAPTER 15

On their way to lunch, Nathalie and Carter passed Mindy coming out of her office. She had not been in morning group, and this was the first Carter had seen her since Saturday night. She wore a plain, woven skirt, baggy wool sweater, brand new Birkenstocks—the suede odor still fresh—with wool socks bunched at the ankles. All earth tones.

"New outfit?" Nathalie asked.

Mindy twirled, as though the back of the shapeless skirt and baggy sweater looked any different from the front. "My new look."

"Has tree hugging replaced feminism?" Carter asked.

"I needed a new image," Mindy said to Nathalie, pulling at the sleeves of her sweater with her palms.

Since the hour and their destination were obvious, Carter invited Mindy to join them for lunch. "You can eat vegetarian at Saint Phoenix. They're very politically correct."

"I am not a vegetarian," she told him, with a touch of

contempt. "Besides, I have other plans."

Just then her other plans walked around the corner. "Ready?" Dana asked.

"Let me get my purse."

Dana gave Nathalie and Carter a wink. "Nonsense. I asked, my treat."

"Dana, it's the nineties," Mindy said. "Women pay their own way."

"As you wish. I am unaccustomed to these nuances myself."

A rare moment, Mindy did not have a retort.

•••

When Carter returned from lunch, Judy and Howard confronted him outside the boys' shower. Howard shook his head and poked his glasses up his nose. "He won't listen."

A muffled sound echoed off the tiled walls within. Judy, frantically pulling at her fingers, said, "He won't come out. Do something."

Carter found Oscar with his head bent into his arms, forearms against the wall.

"What is it?" Carter asked gently.

Oscar ignored him. His body quivered with fury.

He lurched. Carter jumped back. Oscar's fist slammed against the wall. The skin split and streaked the tiles with blood.

"That was my dad!"

He struck the wall with forceful blows. The sound echoed off the tiles.

"That was my dad," he repeated with each blow.

His fury focused on the raw violence of his fist. It exploded over and over into the tiles.

Carter stood by helplessly and watched Oscar flail at the wall. For a split instant, he saw Kelly flailing at their mom. He had just stood and watched.

Oscar's fist thudded into the wall.

Stop! Carter wanted to shout but couldn't. All he could feel was Oscar's fury.

Eventually, Oscar exhausted himself and slumped against the wall.

"What is it?"

Oscar looked at Carter, his eyes open wounds. "They didn't bust me at White Castle. When that wino started to bleed, I freaked, but I didn't run. I couldn't move."

Tears swelled in his eyes. He wiped them with his fist, smearing his forehead with blood. "He left when I was six. I used to see him every now and then, meet him at the corner with a bottle I'd stolen for him. That was when he was still just my old man. But after a few years, I realized what he really was. A bum. I stopped meeting him. I didn't see him for years. I didn't know if he was even alive. But I saw him once last winter in line at the Catholic Charities across town.

He looked all stooped and broken, unshaven, wearing only one shoe. He was a mess. I walked away."

He spoke in a firm, scratched whisper. His wounded eyes showed all the emotion hidden from his voice.

"When I saw that wino bleeding in the alley, I saw my old man. It overcame me, this obsession: *He needs help.* I was possessed. I carried him on my shoulders all the way to the hospital. I was shouting and screaming at the attendants because they didn't care. That's when the cop nabbed me."

He paused.

"I didn't mean to hurt him." He slammed his fist again into the wall. "He shouldn't have died."

"You were high that night?"

"Wasted."

"Would you have hurt him if you hadn't been?"

He slammed his fist one last time against the tiles. The blood dripped like tears from his knuckles.

From the way Oscar looked at him, Carter could tell the compassion showed in his eyes and Oscar saw it. Their eyes embraced.

"Let's get that hand taken care of."

Oscar cradled his broken right fist in his left arm like a baby and let Carter steer him by the elbow down to the emergency room.

•••

Carter left Oscar downstairs while he was fitted with a cast—he had fractured several bones—and went straight to Nathalie's office. She was just finishing a phone call and motioned for Carter to sit down.

"Okay, yes."

"Mm hmm. Thanks again, Alison. Give my love to Brendan."

"Right. You, too."

The whole time, she was grinning at Carter. Before she had replaced the receiver, she said, "We're all set. There's a consultant in Wisconsin right now, so he can be here tomorrow morning. Not only that, but—our luck—he happens to be Sister X's supervisor."

"That should satisfy Dana."

"Also, Mindy's with us. Dana told me she said something like, 'She's a disgrace.' They must've had a wicked lunch."

"Plotting Sister X's assassination? I'm sure."

"Whoa, what got into you?"

He told her about Oscar. "I know it sounds crazy, but somehow it felt like I was in there beating that wall myself."

Before Nathalie could respond, Judy buzzed on the intercom. "Carter in there?"

"No," he said.

"Sister Xavier wants to see you."

Nathalie and Carter looked at each other curiously. Neither

one had seen her since Saturday night. "About?"

"She didn't say."

Carter didn't believe Judy. She usually knew everything that went on, especially if there was some secrecy to it. "Anything to do with Saturday night?"

"She didn't say."

"I'll be right there."

Judy clicked off. Carter asked Nathalie, "What do I say if she asks me about Saturday night?"

"Tell her the truth."

"Sure, make me the martyr."

"Let me know if they play hockey in heaven."

"Very funny."

Carter found Sister Xavier in her high-backed leather chair swiveled toward the window. The sky hung low and gray. She stared into the depths of the river below, supporting her head between her hands. Her expression was recovering from a wince, probably from barking "Entrez!" too loudly.

"Carter, you have been a good employee," she began, still staring into the river. "I have never had any trouble with you."

Her praise hung on a disclaimer. Carter searched for some clue as to how Saturday night was to be interpreted, but she offered none.

She swiveled to face him. "What's this I hear about Oscar?"

Judy had not wasted any time in getting the news to her.

That confirmed his instinct not to let Judy know Dana's plan.

"He was a little upset. He's calmed down."

Sister X leaned forward suddenly. "A little—"

The sudden motion made her wince again. She slowly poured herself a glass of water from the pitcher on her desk. After she had settled her headpiece back against the chair, she started over. "Slamming his fist against the wall. Being treated in the ER. You call this a *little* upset?"

"He got honest. That upset—angered—him. But he's making progress." He added involuntarily, "You'll be pleased."

"Carter, we have a deal. That boy will make it. But without any more scenes. Understand?"

He nodded, annoyed.

"The fundraiser turned out well. What we made will tide us over for about two months, but we still need this arrangement with the county to work. They could keep us supplied with enough referrals to break even. Any kids beyond that spell profits for HQ. I must be able to show them our test case has been worth the risk."

So, they could call the fundraiser a success and leave it at that, Carter figured. He nodded again, angry at his complicity.

The first week Carter had been at Six West, Sister Mary Xavier had taken him out to lunch. During the meal, they had discussed his past work experience and the history of the unit. He had expected as much: the lunch was an extension of his interview. But then, over coffee—actually, coffee for him, another martini for her (her third, or was it her fourth?)—she started talking spontaneously about herself.

She had been a student in Paris, researching and writing her dissertation on Saint Catherine Labouré. Has he heard of her? Is the College of Saint Catherine named after her? No, that's Catherine Benincasa, an Italian. Catherine Labouré was a French visionary. She had seen the Blessed Mother. "What greater tribute, I'd thought, than to have the Mother of God revealed to you? I'd seen Zoé—that was her childhood nickname—as a spiritual hero. I went to Paris to learn all I could about this holy girl and her apparitions.

"I was merely a naïve and innocent girl myself." Sister Xavier prods about her martini with the yellow plastic sword that skewered two olives. "I used to walk from my room in Montparnasse to the Chapelle Notre Dame de la Médaille Miraculeuse, this tiny little church off rue du Bac where Zoé had her visions back in 1830."

She unclasps a medallion from around her neck hidden beneath her suit—he hadn't noticed the slim silver chain—and passes it to him. "That's the miraculous medallion. Zoé said the Virgin told her to have it made."

Carter turns the medallion, the size of a silver dollar, over in his hand. On one side is the design of a moon and three crosses, on the other the inscription: *Ô Marie, conçue sans péché, priez pour nous qui avons recours à vous.*

She sips her martini. "I used to pray to her there at the side of the altar."

"To Mary?"

"To Zoé. Her body is preserved inside a glass casket. Still looked so young." Her tone sounds envious.

Sister X shakes her headpiece and drains her martini. "She died young, a virgin, a model of fidelity to her faith in Mary."

She plucks the plastic sword out of the empty glass and studies it a moment. "I met a Frenchman myself one night at a soirée."

She slides one of the olives off the sword between her teeth. She chews the olive. Carter chews his tongue.

She had seen him before at the school; he remembered her. He was French, he was older. He was charming. She had been drinking, perhaps too much that evening, but everything had seemed so right: the soirée, the wine, the Frenchman. He seduced her; she was careless.

Her eyes glaze out of focus. Carter has seen this look: when Mom reaches a certain level of intoxication where she makes promises that she will not remember. He raises his coffee cup, realizes it's empty, and returns it to the saucer.

"I haven't told anyone this." She reaches out her hand and lays it on his, stroking it clumsily. "I can trust you, can't I?"

He nods dumbly, embarrassed. He shifts in his chair, her

hand still resting on his.

"I knew right away I was pregnant. When I told him, he accused me of betraying him and left. I didn't even know his last name."

She slides off the second olive between her teeth.

"What did you do?"

"I had an abortion."

She says it offhandedly, chewing the olive. Carter expects her to tear up or cross herself or something. But she says it so matter-of-factly—"I called the carpet cleaners," or "I had my hair done"—that it startles him. He senses there is more emotion underneath that refuses to be so casually sloughed off. She orders another martini.

He is at a loss for what she expects him to say. If he can keep her talking, he won't have to say anything. "So then you joined the convent?"

"The convent sent me to study in Paris. If they ever found out, even now, they would send me off to the Des Moines house. That's our order's version of Siberia."

She gazes at him for a long moment. He sees the deep emptiness in her eyes, like staring down a dry well. He can feel her pain swell in his own stomach. "I failed my Zoé. I was not worthy of her."

She takes a long drink from her fresh martini. "I lacked her fidelity to the life of prayer. I lost hope in the lives of the saints, but my consolation was to make the most of this one. I would make myself a success in this world, since that was all I had left. I never went back to see Zoé. Even she could not forgive me."

She withdraws her hand from his, takes back the medallion, and clasps it about her neck, slipping it under her suit.

"You didn't leave?"

She slurps her martini. "I couldn't. I had committed myself."

She fishes a cigarette from her purse. "Do you mind?"

"No," he lies.

She places it between her lips and leans forward for him to light it.

In the weeks that followed, Carter looked to her for some sign of remembrance from their lunch—a knowing look, a veiled hint—but received none. She acted as if it had never happened.

"One more thing," Sister Xavier said. Her hands massaged her temples. "I just got a call from HQ telling me we're scheduled for a visit from a consultant. What can you tell me about that?"

He could taste the seduction in her tone. He steeled himself against it. "Nothing."

She studied him for a moment, her blue eyes slightly puzzled, but the effort seemed too much for her, and she turned back to the river. "That will be all. No more scenes."

On his way out, Carter swung the massive wooden door shut harder than necessary and smiled at its enormous thud.

CHAPTER 16

Carter snapped shut Oscar's file. This time he had recorded only what needed to be said, in case Oscar read it again. If he did, though, Carter didn't think he would react the same. The shower wall had opened a chink in his defiance.

Mickey told Carter it was getting late: his little hand scratched his shoes. Carter still needed to find a ride home.

He traced the smell of Nathalie's perfume down the hallway to her office. A stack of charts crowded her desk. She scribbled in one.

"Mind if I interrupt, Ms. Mead?"

"Carter, you came to finish up for me?"

"I came to steal a cup of coffee." He held up the nearly empty pot. "Want some?"

"Finish it."

He poured the dregs into a Styrofoam cup. "I took your advice."

"You're going ahead with the lobotomy?"

"Funny. I brought my car into the garage. Actually, they came and got it. Wouldn't start this morning."

"You finally broke through your denial."

"I liked denial—it saved me money. So, I need a ride home tonight. Any takers?"

"I've got to pick up Terry from play practice then go to aerobics. It's the other way. But I could give you a ride home after that. Want to come watch?"

"Do you have one of those hot Lycra outfits?"

"The hottest. Terry would like the company."

"I've got a hockey game myself."

"I thought you played on Friday nights."

"Tonight's open ice, just pick-up, but I want to skate."

"Your loss. On a serious note, how's your mother?"

"Checked on her this afternoon. She was sleeping. The nurse told me no change."

"Still detoxing?"

"Far as I know."

Carter sipped the burnt coffee. Outside Nathalie's curtained windows, the clouds had broken up some but still hovered low over the river, backlit by the sinking sun.

"I ran into Ernie down there." They knew the hospital chaplain from A.A. meetings at Saint Phoenix. "He brought her communion."

"She Catholic?"

"More or less."

"Practicing?"

"Habitual."

"Didn't you tell me she'd been raised by nuns?"

"As an orphan. They left their imprint on her. She didn't so much lose her faith as get stuck in it. She goes through the routine but without putting any soul into it."

"Ever tell her about the program?"

"She always kept her drinking private. Except for one time she was pulled over by a cop. I'm sure others—outside our family—must've known in a way."

"But you've never talked with her about A.A.?"

"She would never listen."

"How can you know if you haven't tried?"

"I know my mother."

"But you can't know the outcome. That's in God's hands. Your part is simply to make the effort."

"Maybe," he said. "Maybe."

He left Nathalie to finish her charting and continued his search for a ride home. Dana waited for Bruce. They were going out to dinner to celebrate their fifth anniversary. Buddha had already left. Even Judy had gone, though Carter would have taken the bus before asking her for a ride. That left Mindy.

He feared she was still sore about Saturday evening, but she surprised him by saying yes, and not in a superior way that would render him indebted to her, but almost happily, glad to help. She had a skirt to drop off at the cleaners over that way anyway, only it was at home. Would he mind if they stopped at her place first? Not at all.

They walked to her car in the ramp, her Birkenstocks scuffing the concrete floor. "I think Sister X knows something's up," Carter said. "She asked me if I knew anything about the HQ consultant."

"The HQ person will be here tomorrow, right? We'll get her before she can get us."

"You make it sound like a witch hunt."

"Don't get me started."

"On what?"

"The way men have used that term to brand women as evil. It goes back to Salem—"

"Okay, I won't get you started. If Dana's plan fails, though, we could all be immediately unemployed."

"She's the one who should be unemployed. I've lost all respect for her. If I were her supervisor, after Saturday night she would be finished, end of career. I'd see to it."

Despite his earlier anger at Sister X, Carter found himself defending her. "Mindy, she can't just be discarded. She's an alcoholic."

"That's why she would be finished."

"She deserves help. She might refuse it, but she should at

least be given the chance."

"Now you're going to tell me it's a disease and not her fault. Love the sinner, not the sin. I know. I've read all about it. But how can what she did Saturday night not be her fault? She did it. She drank that much. No one else did that. No one made her do that."

"The disease did."

She said in a mocking tone, "The devil made me do it."

"Well—"

"Don't get me started on *that*."

"Maybe she's never seen help as available."

"Carter, of course she knows help is available. She works in a treatment center."

"I mean maybe she's too close to it. She hasn't seen how it applies to *her*. She's never understood how treatment works, the spiritual side, that is."

"I would think that as a nun she might have some insight into the spiritual side of things."

"I'm not so sure about that."

They arrived at Mindy's car, a once white, now rusting, Datsun 210 parked in the section reserved for doctors.

"I'm glad my tetanus shot is current," Carter quipped.

"Would you rather walk?"

"Nice car. Rust is my favorite color."

Mindy climbed in and unlocked the passenger door from

the inside. As Carter started to get in, she quickly scooped several magazines off the seat and tossed them on the floor in the back. He glimpsed *Cosmopolitan* and *Mademoiselle*. Before he could say anything, she blurted, "They belong to a friend."

"Your boyfriend?"

"They're not completely trash."

"No, the covers are nice to look at."

"Not what I mean. There are things about women men don't understand that need to be written about in women's magazines. It's like having a friend to confide in who also confides in you, someone who knows everything about you without you having to say it all."

He still saw the magazines as part of her fantasy of herself, as though by imagination alone she could transform her short body into that of the long-legged model on the cover. "Some friend."

Her expression told him he had gone too far.

"Just kidding."

"Don't patronize me."

He shut up. Silence was safest. Perhaps he had pushed her a little too far, a little too hard, like children play-fighting when one hits the other a little too authentically, making the other cry.

She drove carelessly, taking long looks at the drivers of the cars she passed, checking her teeth in the mirror, turning to Carter—paying attention to just about everything but the traffic.

"You're one of those men who will never understand women."

"I know women only too well. Believe me."

"You only think you do. That's why you'll never understand them."

"Is this what I don't understand?" He retrieved one of the magazines and flipped to the table of contents. "They're all about men, anyway: 'What He Feels During Sex,' 'Unlock His Inner Teddy Bear,' 'Rate Your Man—Is He a Giver or a Taker?' So what would I be?"

"You're a taker."

"Wrong. I'm happy if she's happy."

"That's just it. You want to please her so you can feel good."

"Nothing wrong with feeling good."

"But you can't until she does. You're probably one of those men who politely gives the woman her orgasm first so you can fall asleep after your turn."

"I'm flawed because I like to satisfy a woman sexually? I'll bet there are a lot of women who could happily accept that flaw in me."

"At a price. You obligate them to reciprocate."

"Listen to Doctor Ruth."

"Ever had a woman just lie back and say thanks?"

"They usually return the favor."

"Out of obligation. The taker enslaves those he loves. They are bound to him—rather, he seeks to bind them to him—by the obligation of returning his love. That's the price they must pay in appreciation." Mindy spoke animatedly, her cheeks flushed, her words coming faster. "The giver, on the other hand, gets pleasure out of giving. He loves without expecting anything in return; he gives freely."

"But he—or *she*—gets pleasure out of it. That makes him-slash-her a taker, too."

"That's not *why* he gives. The pleasure of giving for him is incidental. He gives for the other. You don't love people. You indenture them."

"Damn, when you're done taking my inventory, may I have it back?"

Mindy fiddled with the Suzanne Vega cassette in the tape deck. They approached a red light at full speed, the car in front of them slowed. "The problem with takers—"

"Look out!"

She slammed the brake. They skidded within inches of the bumper in front of them. "Sorry," she said, reluctantly.

He wasn't finished. "I suppose men are the only ones with these problems according to your friend *Cosmo*?"

"Of course there are women who struggle with the giving/taking issue. I'm probably one. I was raised to be a good girl. That meant don't think of yourself, which doesn't lead to giving but to repression. The reaction, unfortunately, has been to the other extreme: too much taking." She flicked her eyes at the rearview mirror. "I've been doing a lot of thinking since Saturday night."

Her honesty surprised Carter. He had not thought her capable of such insights independent of a textbook. There was more awareness behind her baffled air than he realized.

"What about the others, any givers among them?"

"Buddha, Nathalie."

"Dana?"

"Maybe with Bruce, certainly with the kids, but not with the staff."

"Judy, Howard—takers?"

"Easily."

"Sister X?"

She pondered that for a moment. "Taker."

"Not what you would have said before Saturday."

"Today's a new day."

They reached her apartment without further incident. Mindy lived in student housing at the university, a small, one-bedroom on the third floor of a generic sixties era apartment building. Rather than wait in the cold car staring at the alley dumpsters, Carter accepted her invitation to come upstairs while she fetched her skirt. Slipping into the bedroom, she called over her shoulder, "I'll just be a minute."

Carter waited in the kitchen doorway and surveyed the apartment: postcard of a naked Chippendales-type man taped to the refrigerator, bowl of half-eaten popcorn on the counter, brown beanbag chair with a book open on the floor next to it, makeshift bookcase of cinder blocks and unpainted pine boards, two Georgia O'Keefe prints on the wall. (*Are they or aren't they? Mindy said they aren't because Georgia O'K said they aren't. They are*, Carter thought. *Nothing that obvious could be accidental or incidental.*)

A fat black-and-white cat walked with short and clumsy steps out of the bedroom.

"That's Gloria," Mindy called.

"As in Steinham?"

"Who else?"

Of course, he thought.

The cat waddled past, glanced at him, settled into the bean bag, and closed her eyes, indifferent.

He started singing, "G-L-O-R-I-A, Glooor-ia!"

The cat did not open her eyes.

Restless, Carter absentmindedly opened one of the cupboard doors: Chef Boyardee Spaghettios; Orville Redenbacher popcorn; Campbell's chicken with stars soup; three cans of Friskies cat food—turkey with gravy; and a box of Carnation chocolate chip breakfast bars. At lunch one day in the cafeteria, when Nathalie complained about the hospital food, Mindy had made the case that cooking had kept women imprisoned in the kitchen. "The task of feeding their husbands and families is the true opiate of the female masses," she had pontificated. Obviously, she had resisted this enslavement. And, Carter thought looking into the cupboard, this was the price she paid for her emancipation.

•••

Mindy dropped him off at the garage. They charged him $220 for a new coil, but he was relieved to have his car fixed. He made it to his hockey game, which he thought he might miss. His side won, and he scored two goals but didn't think he played well. He had looked forward to the sensation of simply skating fast and freely across the ice. Instead, his legs felt wooden and sluggish. Once home, he fixed a late meal of fettuccini alfredo and a Caesar salad, ate ravenously, then settled into his bath. Mindy's words came back to him: "You don't love people; you indenture them." *That's not just me, that's Mom, too.*

He slept fitfully. She called to him, "Carter, would you come here a minute?" When he opened the door, Mindy stood astride the sink in a skirt and black lace bra that looked a size too small the way it pushed her breasts out of the cups. His eyes traced the rounded upper edge of her nipples.

"I wanted to try this on before I brought it in, make sure

it still fits. Will you zip me up?"

She turned her back to him, the zipper resting on her buttocks. Seeing the zipper as just pulled down rather than waiting to be pulled up, and glimpsing the black lace panties exposed in the skirt's open slit, aroused him unexpectedly. His eyes slid up the curve of her spine to the flesh between her neck and shoulders, a smooth, tender slope.

He reached for the zipper, steadied his other hand on her bottom, and teased it upward slowly. She turned to face him—his lower hand came to rest on her hip—and peered at him from underneath her thick eyelashes. "Thank you," she said, her breath on his chest.

He stood motionless, lost in the sensation, unable to turn away, yet hesitant to move forward.

"I think this bra is too small," she said, reaching back and unfastening its hook. She squirmed out of the bra, her generous breasts dropping freely before him.

That proved to be his undoing.

Carter tossed and turned to the thudding sounds of the couple upstairs. He lay awake in the narrow twin bed while Mindy dozed, her breath falling deep and easy. Outside, a warm wind blew. He could hear the weekend's snow starting to melt, dripping against the windowsill. Mindy's arm lay heavily against his chest and cramped his breath. He studied her body next to his. Short legs, small feet, pudgy toes. Full breasts and a head two sizes too big for her body. For the first time, he saw the distortion of her body clearly. It looked funny, the way a word does when you stare at it for too long.

He experienced a sudden flash of clarity. In the lucid release that follows climax, he saw that the things he had told himself earlier when he wanted her were not true. Yes, Mindy's breasts were ample, but they were out of place. He could not find her sexy, especially with her lying naked next to him. Only moments earlier, she had been all he wanted; now, she was considerably less.

An icicle crashed against the drainpipe outside and snapped him awake from a dream about his mother. She had been scratching his back in her bed. He had promised to build a church for her: Saint Elizabeth's.

Carter saw again the distorted shape of Mindy's body. Her breasts rose and fell evenly with her breath. Despite her arm across his chest, she was not holding him there. He was. He was free to leave any time. The memory of the texture of her round, brown nipples on his tongue stirred the desire to stay. He could hear the lies he told himself earlier in the evening whispering in his ears. He wanted to climb out of the bed but could not move, as in a dream when the legs won't respond to the command to run. The bed was a quicksand sucking him in. He could feel the taste of Mindy's nipples swallowing him. *God, save me!* he cried.

And awoke. The bed sheets had entangled his legs.

He tried to dismiss it all as a dream, but knew that it was part of him, that he couldn't just cast it off because he hadn't been conscious.

CHAPTER 17

Rodney was scheduled to graduate Tuesday. His friendship with Oscar had blossomed quickly. After Oscar's first weekend, as a sign of their friendship, Rodney had tried to give Oscar his gypsum arrowhead necklace, but Oscar had refused the gift. Tuesday morning, they came out of their room wearing each other's jackets. Rodney, in Oscar's faded and worn jean jacket, the Guns 'N Roses patch emblazoned across the back, looked hard and more ragged than usual. The day before, Carter had not been able to imagine Rodney, ever mellow and solemn, slapping his girlfriend, but seeing him in Oscar's mangy jacket, he suddenly could.

Oscar, on the other hand, who had not been a moment without his jean jacket, seemed calmer in Rodney's jacket. The fringes swung easily on his back, like his hair over his shoulders. The brown suede softened the features of his face.

Upon seeing the two that morning, Carter couldn't help but think that he was seeing a sheep in wolf's clothing and vice versa.

He sipped a cup of coffee with Nathalie and Buddha at the nurses' station, waiting for Mickey to tell them it was time for Rodney's graduation. The kids were still milling about, showering, getting dressed, or eating breakfast. Archie ate potato chips mashed in a cereal bowl with milk. Whitney asked Buddha to fasten a necklace for her, pressing her rump against his thigh as he did. He delicately stepped aside and sent her on her way. Chip practiced his slam shots alone on the foosball table. Oscar sat by the window in his new jacket, looking outside at the dawning day, the dim sky ambivalent, not letting on which way the weather would go.

Sister Xavier strode down the hall with a man who turned out to be the headquarters consultant. She introduced Nathalie, Buddha, Judy, and Carter to Robbie Fletcher. Carter had expected a sunburnt surfer type in banker's clothing—blue suit, club tie, gold watch, wingtips. Instead, Fletcher, who appeared to be mid-thirties, looked like he had stepped out of an L. L. Bean catalog. He wore a forest-green cotton sweater over a plaid flannel shirt; beige, wide wale corduroys; and two-tone (brown and green) Timberlands. He had wavy brown hair that curled past his shoulders, a straight nose, and high cheekbones. When he smiled, he resembled Michael Landon in his role as the benevolent father in *Little House on the Prairie*. He even had a Midwestern accent. Carter figured he would prove the perfect ally for their plan.

Mickey's toe touches told Carter it was 8:30, fifteen minutes to morning group. Regular as clockwork, the kids started to line up at the nurses' station for their morning cigarette break. Judy doled out one cigarette apiece from their packs. Whitney, seeing Sister Xavier, asked about her discharge date. Sister X referred her to Nathalie, her counselor, and prepared to leave. Whitney persisted, "My daddy says I don't have to stay longer than I want."

"That's not your father's decision to make."

"It could be if he wants it to be."

Glancing at Fletcher, Sister X snapped, "We'll see about that."

Fletcher was preoccupied with the kids lighting their cigarettes from the community lighter that hung by a chain from the counter of the nurses' station. He missed Sister Xavier's remark and Whitney's flirtations with him. "How many smoke breaks do they have in one day?"

An incriminating tone animated his question.

"Five," Judy said. "This one in the morning, one after lunch, one in the afternoon, one after supper, and one before bedtime."

"Isn't the hospital smoke-free?"

Sister Xavier answered him, "The administration has allowed us this exception."

The staff had debated this issue themselves eight months ago when the hospital declared itself smoke-free. Nathalie had suggested the unit ask that Six West be given an exemption. She and Carter, though both nonsmokers, argued that taking away cigarettes slowed the treatment process because for the first week, while the kids endured nicotine withdrawal, cigarettes became their focus rather than chemicals. Denying cigarettes exaggerated their importance. Dana, a fanatic runner, and Judy, a purist, had been in favor of enforcing the smoking restriction. Howard went along with Judy. Mindy sided with Nathalie and Carter, citing some theory on behavior modification. Buddha had been neutral. Sister X had cast the deciding vote and secured an exemption from the hospital administration. Now, her CareCorps supervisor was challenging her.

He backed off somewhat at her tone. "Ideally, all CareCorps units would be smoke free. Otherwise, the kids use nicotine as simply another crutch."

"Let's you and I discuss this later."

Fletcher said no more, but the way he returned her stern look let Carter know he was not going to drop the issue.

•••

Usually Nathalie and Carter facilitated the graduation ceremonies by themselves, but Tuesday morning, Dana,

Mindy, Buddha, and even Judy joined them.

Rodney was the kind of kid that made the staff proud. He had come in broken, struggled, and made changes. Through it, he had inspired others. Despite all of the exploitation and selfish intentions behind the scenes, there were still kids who emerged from treatment with a new lease on life. The staff took satisfaction in his growth.

The spectators clustered around the circle of kids seated in the group room. The kids passed around a medallion for Rodney, each taking a turn to hold it and wish him well. Many of them, even the boys—matter of fact, most of the boys—cried when they spoke of Rodney's strong example of doing what he believed right, not in a brownnoser way but more in a you-do-what-you-gotta-do way. They did not use the word integrity, but that is what they meant. Rodney sat solemn and dignified, looking out of place in Oscar's Guns 'N Roses jean jacket, listening closely and modestly to their praise, thanking each one in return. Too bad Sister Xavier didn't get to see this, Carter thought. From it, she might have glimpsed the true meaning of treatment.

When the medallion reached Oscar, he pressed it in the palm of his bandaged hand and rubbed the round coin affectionately with his thumb. He studied its markings and turned it over in his hand: the A.A. triangle on one side with the words "To thine own self be true," and on the other side the Serenity Prayer. He did not speak right away but spent a long moment studying the medallion. Oscar looked to Rodney then down again. He rubbed the medallion with his thumb. A mixture of longing and envy and caring passed over his face. Something in him seemed to be struggling to free itself. He looked back at Rodney sitting across from him, shook his hair back over the shoulders of his new brown suede jacket, and bit his lip. His gaze returned to the medallion. He squeezed it in his palm.

With his eyes fixed on the hand that clutched Rodney's medallion, he finally whispered in his rough voice, "If you don't stay straight, I'm going to kick your ass."

•••

Rodney's mother had not come to his graduation. She could not take the time off from work. But she had agreed to let Rodney return to live with her. His county social worker had attended the ceremony but had left immediately afterward to get over to the courthouse for another case. So Carter drove Rodney home.

Rodney's younger sister and mother lived with her brother and his family just off Franklin Avenue. Coming up the avenue, Carter and Rodney drove under the Hiawatha bridge, past the detox center on one side, the American Indian Center on the other. They passed a group of weathered men huddled on the stone steps of the library next door to Catholic Charities. Across the street was Walgreens, where Rodney's girlfriend worked.

Carter turned left onto 13th Avenue past two men leaned under the open hood of a rusted-out Chevrolet Impala. The broken sidewalks had long been neglected by the city, given up on as being past repair; the lawns were merely lots of muddy snow. A young girl without a jacket played house with a group of shoeless dolls lined up against a chain-link fence.

When Archie had first met Rodney, he hopped about with his fingers to his head as antlers and grunted, "Tatonka."

Rodney hadn't understood.

"You know," Archie said. "*Dances with Wolves.*"

"Never saw it."

"Never saw *Dances with Wolves*? It's all about how great Indian culture is."

"I missed that one."

Rodney's uncle's house was a two-story duplex, the porch listing heavily to one side where a stack of cinder blocks kept it from collapsing. Large sections of brown paint had peeled away to expose the wood siding. Across one window, a row of Lotto Minnesota stickers decorated the pane. As they approached, Carter saw that they sealed a crack in the glass.

They pulled up to the curb, and Rodney, ever solemn and sincere, said, "Thanks for the ride." He climbed out of the car and leaned his head back in the door. "Thanks for everything, Carter. You saved my life."

"You saved your life. I just got to watch. Keep the faith."

He fished the medallion out of his pocket. "I've got it right here."

Carter watched him climb confidently up the porch steps. They sagged under his weight. Still clutching the medallion, Rodney reached for the door with his free hand and entered the house.

CHAPTER 18

Carter returned to the unit just before noon. While he was out, Sister X had mandated that Six West become smoke-free. Judy pointed to the memo taped to the nurses' station counter: "Effective immediately, Six West will conform to the CareCorps smoke-free policy." Maybe she was more vulnerable than they realized, Carter thought. Or, maybe she was willing to bend on the smaller issues to protect the bigger ones.

Nathalie and Carter discussed the implications at the nurses' station.

"The kids aren't going to like it."

"I don't want to be the messenger on this one."

Fletcher strolled down the hall. Nathalie and Carter wanted to maneuver him into one of their offices so they could set up a time to present their case to him but wanted to do so without arousing Judy's suspicion. As they waited for the opportune moment, Nathalie managed to talk him into letting the kids keep their next smoke break so that the ban wouldn't go into effect until late afternoon. He accepted the rationale that it would be best to let the kids finish afternoon group before stirring them up.

Sister Xavier approached. "There you are. Ready for lunch?"

Over her shoulder, Carter spied Dana come around the corner. Dana leaned his forearms on the far end of the countertop. Fletcher informed Sister X of the delay in implementing the smoking ban. She dismissed him with a brush of her hand. "You're the boss."

Dana had not said anything. It was uncharacteristic for him not to have an opinion to express. He had been ominously quiet, leaning on the edge of the counter, a thunderhead on the horizon.

Sister X glanced at him and said to Fletcher, "Let's eat."

As they were about to head off, Dana, nonchalantly rubbed one palm across his forearm, smoothing the hair across it, and asked in a calm, unhurried tone, "Sister Mary Xavier, would you indulge me one question?"

She eyed him impatiently. "What is it?"

"What brand of hairspray do you use?"

"Excuse me?"

"What hairspray do you use?" He stroked his forearm. "Your hair always exhibits such a natural look, as though you did not use any spray at all, yet I know you must because I have smelt it myself so often in your office. One concludes it must be an incredible product. I would like to know, what brand is it?"

Sister Xavier's eyes flamed. "We're going to lunch."

Fletcher followed her down the hall, casting a puzzled look back at Dana.

Nathalie ushered Dana into the nearest office, Carter's. "What was that all about? Couldn't you wait to get her?"

Dana looked like he had just bit the inside off his mouth. "Do you know who that was?"

"Who?"

"That was the man with whom she got sauced Thursday night!"

•••

Carter understood his mother's desire to keep drinking. If he was having a bad day, he got stoned. A good day, he got stoned. If he was pissed off, he got stoned. Happy, he got stoned. Bummed out, sad, hurt, embarrassed, or ashamed—pass the bong. Or the bottle. Whatever was around. If you had asked him then, he would have told you he wouldn't quit because he loved getting high; he didn't want to give that up. After treatment, he would have told you more simply, he had fallen in love with alcohol and pot. A baby dope fiend—that was him. Wasn't hard for him to understand his mom. They were so alike. She was an alcoholic, plain and simple. But he knew if she was going to have any chance at recovery, she needed to admit it herself.

That admission was her only hope, Carter figured. He didn't want to lose her. Maybe she would understand it one alcoholic to another. Or maybe not. But Nathalie was right—he had to try. So, Tuesday after his lunch hour, he stopped down to see her with a bouquet of flowers and a copy of *Alcoholics Anonymous*, the "Big Book."

She didn't look good. Her face was a pale yellow, the color of faded newsprint, and the little spidery blotches on her arms had become more pronounced. She was still chained to the IV at her bedside. Her whole body looked frail and pitiful.

Her eyes followed him from the door to her bedside without her head moving from the pillow. "They won't let me smoke."

Her voice was weak. He had to ask her to repeat herself before he understood what she said.

"I want to get out of here."

"I brought you flowers, Mom. Freesias, lilies of the valley, and baby roses."

He placed the vase on her nightstand and fluffed the arrangement. Several other bouquets and plants filled her little room.

Her eyes seemed to shorten. "Remember when you used to pick me bouquets at the arboretum?"

He sat down on the side of the bed and took her hand. "I'll never forget those days, Mom."

Peering into her eyes was like peering into shallow water—he could see their flat bottom when she said, "That's all that's left now, Carter. Memories."

She coughed. He waited. "How will you remember me, Carter?"

The question caught him off guard. "I want to remember you sober, Mom," he blurted.

"It's too late for that."

When he had entered the room, the distinct hospital stink—a combination of body odor and disinfectant—had hit him. Sitting next to her, though, he detected the smell of cognac.

"Mom, I brought you something else. This book is written by alcoholics. It helped me get sober. I finally realized that if my life was going to get better, it was up to me, no one else. I had to change."

"That hurt us."

"I'm telling you this to let you know I understand the pain you're in."

"How could you understand, Carter? Has this ever happened to you?"

"I felt despair myself. That hole inside that I kept trying to fill."

"After all we gave you. Is that what you've come to tell

me, that I failed you as your mother?"

"Mom, I've come to tell you I love you. You gave me what you could. I want to give back what I can."

She breathed with difficulty. In her wheezes, the scent of cognac was unmistakable. The nurses had told him they had found bottles stashed in her room. They couldn't figure out how she smuggled them in.

"Mom, the doctor says your only chance to get better is to quit drinking."

"Carter, I'm dying."

"That's just it, Mom, this is urgent."

"Let me die in peace."

"Mom, it doesn't have to end this way."

"Let me be."

"You've been drinking, haven't you?"

She turned her head away from him. "It's the only comfort I have left."

"It's killing you."

She stared blankly at the wall.

"Can't you see that?!" he said.

She closed her eyes and said nothing. In the drunken flutter of her eyelids, he saw all the dreams he had formed in the clouds those days at the arboretum pass by, drowned by alcohol.

The fury burned in his throat. Alcohol. Goddamn alcohol.

That pimp. He had made Mom his whore. Then dumped her in a broken, yellowed heap to die.

He stood up. "How did you get it?!"

"Carter, please. Don't make a scene."

His eyes flashed about the room. "Who brought it here? Dad?"

"Leave him out of this."

His eyes fell on the philodendron. He had seen it somewhere before. "That college kid. He sent it up in that philodendron. Didn't he? Didn't he?!"

Her silence confirmed it. The guy with the David Letterman face had been smuggling her Courvoisier in the plants he delivered.

"That creep. Doesn't he know what he's doing?"

His fury came into sharp focus on the face with the gap tooth and crooked bangs. "That fucker." Carter stormed out of his mom's room determined to find him.

He hadn't seen the van he drove—didn't they always drive vans?—but knew he must be from one of the neighborhood liquor stores. Outside, the morning's puddles had frozen. Carter raced defiantly across the ice on the sidewalks to the liquor store up the street. The man behind the counter didn't recognize the guy Carter described. Nor did the man at the next liquor store. Carter hit every liquor store within five blocks of Saint Jude's. No one knew the guy. The longer

Carter searched for him, the sharper his fury became. *That fucker poisoned Mom. She was dying from alcohol—he gave her more. He was killing her. Murdering her.*

His crime was worse than homicide. Torture. He killed her slowly, painfully. From the inside out. "Your type deserves the same," he seethed. "You should suffer, too. You deserve the same, slow torture."

He confronted another liquor store owner. "What do you mean that doesn't sound familiar? This is the last place in the neighborhood. He's got to work here. College age, gap tooth, crooked bangs. No?"

The short, balding man behind the counter spread his palms up. "You're not going to rob me, are you? I been robbed six times the last two months. Times are hard. I know. Hard for all of us. You'll put me out of business. Don't rob me now."

Carter was looking for the guy who was killing his mother, and this guy thought he was going to rob him. *Absurd. Rob him while someone is robbing my mother? That guy has slowly stolen her soul. Delivered her to the devil, alcohol.*

His fury slipped to despair. A swollen, sinking feeling choked off all other sensations. He had been staring blankly over the head of the short, balding man. The bottles slowly came into focus. A powerful genie lurked within those bottles. A genie that could make a timid man dance and a strong man buckle. That could make a fool of wise men and a sage of fools. A genie that was easily summoned but ever so difficult to put back.

"We'll make a deal, you and me," the balding man was saying. "See, I'm a reasonable guy. You can have a bottle of whatever you like. On the house. All you gotta do is just leave peaceable. Nobody gets robbed today."

That genie could take me away.

Before Carter knew what had happened, he was walking out of the store clutching a fifth of Jack Daniel's that the balding man had pressed into his hands.

I can take the afternoon off, call in sick with some excuse. Hell, Mom's dying. I can head over to the park, or back home. No more bullshit on the unit. No more of Mom's pain. No more of my own. The afternoon to myself. Just me and Jack.

He could leave a message with Mindy. She wouldn't ask questions like Judy. If he talked to Nathalie, he would feel guilty. But Mindy might say something to spoil it, too. *Why call? I can explain tomorrow.*

He turned toward the hospital parking ramp, headed for his car. Another voice sounded deep within him. Calm yet firm, barely audible amidst his furious despair: *That's not the answer.* He trudged along the sidewalk. "Fuck you. It'll make me feel better."

Until?

"That's enough."

Then what?

"Who cares?"

Remember that we deal with alcohol—cunning, baffling, powerful.

"Fuck you."

Cunning, baffling, powerful.

"Shut up!"

He realized he had shouted out loud and stopped. "Fuck," he muttered.

There was an A.A. meeting at Saint Phoenix at one o'clock. Mickey told him he had five minutes. He could make it if he hurried.

When he got to Saint Phoenix, he found himself still clutching the bottle of JD. He flung it against the brick wall. The bottle shattered to his satisfaction. But the scent of whiskey taunted him. "Fuck you!"

Cigarette smoke greeted him when he shuffled down the stone steps of the former church and into the back room. Of the twenty or so people seated in the metal folding chairs around the table, there were some students, a few professors, a couple of professionals in ties, Buddha, and an older man, seventy at least, short and squat, wearing unwashed overalls and a Twins cap. A filterless cigarette jutted out of his stained fingers. His face was worn and weathered as the earth. A tuft of hair protruded from each ear. He raised the cigarette to cracked lips and inhaled feebly.

Carter remembered the first time he had seen Ernie at a meeting. After looking him over, he had immediately written him off and turned his attention to the other, more learned types. Later in the meeting, they discussed the Eleventh Step ("Sought through prayer and meditation to improve our conscious contact with God, *as we understood him*, praying only for knowledge of his will for us and the power to carry that out") and the others repeated comments routinely offered about the step. Ernie, who had been quiet until then, rolling one cigarette while he smoked another, said during a lull, "I have just two prayers. In the morning, when I wake up, I say to God, 'Surprise me.' In the evening, when I lay my head on the pillow, I say, 'Thank you.'"

In that simple statement, Ernie had taught Carter all he needed to know about the Eleventh Step. He had also taught him that he had something to learn from every alcoholic in the room.

The topic of the meeting Tuesday was the Third Step ("Made a decision to turn our will and our lives over to the care of God, *as we understood him*"). The storm raging in Carter's head made it difficult for him to follow the discussion. He still wanted to strangle the delivery boy.

When it came his turn to speak, he almost stood up to leave. *Fuck it, Mom's dying, let's get drunk.* But something made him stay.

"I want to drink today," he said. "Almost did. I had a bottle of Jack Daniel's in my hand. I wanted to get drunk. Still do. Just get shit-faced and forget the pain."

Saying that strengthened the desire. He could taste the whiskey in his nostrils. Yet, at the same time, there was a relief from admitting his thoughts instead of keeping them stashed in his head.

"Me, too," said one of the professor-looking guys in a tweed jacket and wire-rimmed bifocals. "I did. Took me six years of hell to get sober again."

"So did I," said a thirty-something woman in a floral-print housedress. "I thought I could control it again. I failed. And how. This time around I realized I would only make it if I surrendered."

"Whatever it is making you want to drink won't get any better if you do," Buddha said.

Carter pondered their words. Yet that urge to chase away his pain still nagged him.

"Nothing more natural for an alcoholic than to drink," Ernie said. His stubby fingers raised a hand-rolled cigarette to his lips. "'Course, nothing more natural than alcohol killing an alcoholic, too."

Hearing that fortified the firm voice inside Carter. But he still felt the brunt of his anger.

After the meeting, he stood with Buddha and Ernie in the Saint Phoenix parking lot. He knew there was more he had to say. The fury had clutched his throat. "It's my mom. I spent the morning with her. She's so stubborn. Do you know she's been having a delivery guy smuggle bottles in for her?"

Buddha placed his beefy paw on Carter's shoulder.

The touch snapped something inside of Carter. Tears blurred the vision of her in his mind. Beautiful before her vanity mirror slurred into bruised eyes sitting on the side of his bed. Hair radiant in the sunlight became mouth contorted by coughs and pasty forehead against the pillow. "She's dying—dying from it, fucking dying—but she won't quit," he managed between sobs.

Buddha moved in and smothered him in a bear hug. Carter sank into his embrace. "I miss her."

"I know," Buddha said. "I know."

And Carter knew he did, one alcoholic to another, he did.

"Let yourself breathe."

Buddha's calm consumed Carter. He was able to breathe through the tears. He stepped from his arms, and the air felt fresh on his wet face.

"That's it." Ernie nodded. "You're letting go. That's how we do 'Thy will be done.'"

"I once watched my brother beat her. I didn't stop him. I didn't want to. I thought she had it coming for all she had done to us. I wanted to see him hurt her. It was as though I hit her myself."

"All in God's memory now," Ernie said. "You love her. It's forgiven."

Carter's breath came more smoothly. The air tasted sweet and fresh.

He walked back to the hospital, Buddha on one side of him, Ernie on the other. On the way, Carter noticed the sky had cleared to a pale blue, the color of a robin's egg. Trees he had not noticed on previous walks along this familiar route took shape, each with its own distinct personality. Birds in their bare branches sang to them as they passed. The air tasted sweet.

CHAPTER 19

The afternoon was business as usual. Sister Xavier and Fletcher kept to themselves. Dana moped. Judy charted. The kids attended their daily health lecture then group. Chip again refused to do his First Step; Whitney volunteered that she had been sexually abused but wouldn't say by whom.

Following group, the kids gathered at the nurses' station for their scheduled cigarette break, unaware that Sister X had cancelled their smoking privileges. Archie, regular as a cuckoo clock, announced, "Four-thirty, time for smokes."

Nathalie and Carter had followed the kids out of the group room talking about Chip's resistance, forgetting that this was the fateful hour Six West was to go smoke-free. Down the hall, Dana was telling Buddha about his most recent 10K race. Sister X and Fletcher happened around the corner to collect some charts for Fletcher to review.

Judy told Archie, "No cigarettes this afternoon. Today, Six West joins the rest of the hospital in becoming smoke-free."

"Bad joke, Judy. Give me my cigarette."

The other kids had lined up behind Archie for their cigarettes. Sister X and Fletcher stood to the side, letting Judy face the danger alone.

"It's no joke, Archie. No cigarettes today. No cigarettes tomorrow. No cigarettes no more. We are smoke-free."

"They're my cigarettes. You can't tell me I can't have them."

"Easy does it. It's for your own health. Think of the favor that we—you—will be doing your lungs."

Archie appealed to the other kids. "No more cigarettes. Say it's not so."

He rolled his eyes, yanked at his hair, stomped his foot. The other kids, slightly taken aback by Archie's display, were not sure how to respond.

Until Oscar said, "Archie's right. You can't take away our cigs."

He pulled a cigarette from the fringed pocket of his new jacket and flashed it at Judy. "Wanna try to take this one away, bitch?"

"That's a day drop for contraband," Judy said automatically. She uncapped a marker to record the consequence on the level board behind her. "And a check for profanity."

Nathalie and Carter moved to separate the kids for a time out. Carter shepherded Archie, Chip, and the other boys to the group room; Nathalie led Whitney and the girls the other away. Archie broke apart and rushed after Oscar into room 612. Dana tried to reason with Archie from the doorway, but he was too far gone. He kept shouting from Oscar's room, "No way! No way!"

He suddenly darted out of the room, brushing Dana aside, and scampered over the counter of the nurses' station. He tugged furiously at the padlock on the cabinet. "Gimme my cigarettes!"

Buddha, moving with surprising quickness for someone his size, wrapped his beefy arms around Archie and lifted him off the ground. In the process, Buddha also squeezed his strawberry shake, which dripped down the boy's shirt. Archie struggled mightily but was no match for Buddha's grip.

From the other end of the counter, Sister Xavier and Fletcher gaped in shock.

Oscar appeared from his room, the cigarette now lit and dangling from his lips. He brandished a metal towel rack in his bandaged hand and approached the nurses' station. "I want the rest of my cigarettes."

"You're threatening me," Judy said, still standing at the level board, armed with her uncapped marker. "That's a day drop."

"I'll do more than threaten you, if you don't open that goddamn cabinet. NOW!"

He smashed the metal rack against the countertop. The wood splintered.

"Judy," Carter said. "Back off."

She trembled behind the counter. "He's threatening me."

Nathalie had returned from the girls' quarters. Carter motioned to her with his eyes to take Judy away. Nathalie had already moved two steps toward her. "We'll take care of the consequences later," she told Judy. "Come with me."

She gently escorted Judy down the hall. Judy kept looking back at Oscar, terror twisting her expression.

Carter faced Oscar. Cigarette clenched between his lips. The metal rack glistened in the boy's bandaged hand.

The other boys mobbed around the showdown. They were already angry, dry timber waiting for the spark to set them off. Mindy and Dana watched helplessly. Sister Xavier, appalled, walked Fletcher down the hallway. Carter stood between Oscar and a riot. His knees twitched.

Oscar smacked the rack into his palm. "Open the cabinet."

His eyes glinted fiercely. They betrayed no recognition.

Carter looked to Buddha, who still smothered Archie with his flab, and drew strength.

Instinctively, he knew he could not reason with Oscar's rage. *Breathe*, he told himself.

With each breath, Carter reached toward the serenity deep within himself. A graceful calm spread throughout him. He gazed deep into Oscar's eyes, pressed aside their hard flat exterior, and searched for the tenderness he had seen earlier.

"Open the cabinet, asshole."

Carter breathed in. Peace. He fixed the message in his mind, transmitted it across the taut line of their vision. *Peace.*

Slowly, he reached out his hand. Drops of sweat trickled down his side.

Oscar flinched and raised the rack halfway, cocking his arm, ready to slash away the outstretched hand, but hesitated.

Carter searched for some admission of their intimacy.

"Oscar," he said gently, delicately, a term of endearment. Hand still outstretched, he took a small step toward him.

"Get back, asshole," Oscar growled.

But Carter saw the wound flicker in his eyes.

"Oscar." Again gently, delicately. Soothingly, rhythmically. He stretched his palm farther.

Oscar's shoulders slumped. The smoke from the tip of the cigarette clouded his eyes.

"Oscar. Give me the rack."

Oscar looked intently back at Carter. The fight slowly drained out of his expression. His hand lowered the rack to his side. It slid from his grip and clattered on the floor. With his good hand, he pinched the cigarette from his lips, stubbed it out on the countertop, and surrendered it to Carter's outstretched hand.

He turned and walked slowly past the huddle of bewildered boys to his room.

CHAPTER 20

"Carter, you let me down."

Sister Xavier paced behind her desk. He sat in one of the stiff stuffed chairs. "We had a deal, remember? No more scenes."

She stopped and faced him, hands on the back of her chair. "No more scenes! Remember?"

She resumed her pacing. "You let that situation get out of hand. Robbie did not witness the entire scene, thank God, but he saw enough. He had been willing to go along with it, too, was starting to like the idea, talking about how they could implement it at other CareCorps adolescent units."

Her sharp blue eyes glared accusingly at Carter. "You cost us plenty."

Carter knew he could not defend himself.

"I want you to discharge him."

"Oscar?"

"The troublemaker. Yes."

"He'll get sent up to Rock Lake. Think of what that will

do to him. You know that once kids wind up in the system they rarely get out. Six West is his last chance."

"He should've thought of that before he started smashing things. Send him back to Juvenile."

"He belongs here."

"No, he does not. I've already worked it out. We will say he was not appropriate for our setting because he was not chemically dependent. We will ask the county for a juvenile who is to be our test case."

"He most certainly is chemically dependent. He fits at least six of the *DSM-III* criteria. I've documented it." If they discharged Oscar on the grounds that he wasn't chemically dependent after documenting that he was, the state Department of Health could close the unit for malpractice. Sister X knew Carter knew this. For once, he was grateful for the charts and glad that he had taken the time to rewrite the pages Oscar had shredded. "He belongs here as much as any kid."

Her voice remained firm. "We cannot keep him after the scene he made today."

"Today was progress."

"Progress?! We don't have other kids inciting riots as they make progress. You've got a strange sense of progress, Carter."

Her tone softened. "I know you've become attached to him. Perhaps that clouds your judgment. Think of it in terms of what's best for the whole unit. We need this system of referrals to work out so Six West can survive. You and I agree on that, don't we, that we ought to do what's best for the whole unit?"

"Oscar is the unit. As much as any of the other kids here."

She stood behind her chair, unmoved. "Carter, this is not negotiable. I will not allow one kid to threaten the financial welfare of my unit. Oscar must go. You will amend your entries in his chart. Your final entry will read that we're dismissing Oscar on the grounds that he is not chemically dependent."

Carter stood up. "This is not about budgets or figures you'll put in your annual report. We're talking about a kid's life. The soul of this unit is at stake. He's placed his in our hands. He has trusted us with that. I will not betray him."

Her blue eyes glared at him from across her desk. "Are you defying me?"

"I will not betray him."

"Very well, if Oscar is not gone tomorrow morning, you will be."

She sat down at her desk and began to shuffle papers, no longer regarding him. "I will work it out with the county to send us another adolescent."

She drummed her fingers on the desk. "That will be all."

CHAPTER 21

Tuesday evening, faced with the prospect of unemployment the next day, an ordinary bath did not seem enough. Carter sought the extra relief of a whirlpool. Usually he went to the Uptown YWCA, frequented by men with ponytails and women with tattoos. Last Saturday, he had received in the mail a membership promotion—one week FREE!—at the Calhoun Beach Club, the tony fitness center housed in the classic, turn-of-the-century brick tower overlooking Lake Calhoun. In its parking lot, his '82 Prelude stood conspicuously out of place among the BMWs, Mercedes-Benzes, and Porsches.

The whirlpool rested under a white trellis surrounded by classical statues. Carter soaked in its soothing waters. The gushing jets washed away the worries of the day, relaxed the muscles that had knotted in his shoulders, and cleansed his mind. He alternated between lounging in the whirlpool and swimming a couple of laps in the cool water of the pool. A peaceful resolve to follow his conscience, come what may, filled him. He emerged as refreshed as those who bathed in the waters of Bethesda.

He dressed leisurely. Even the Calhoun Beach Club locker room smelled good. The YWCA locker room reeked of sweaty farts and moldy shower tiles; whiffs of spice deodorant and fruity aftershave scented the CBC locker room. After the near-naked bliss of the whirlpool, Carter was in no hurry to dress and rush back into the world. He wanted to linger in the luxury of this good feeling.

The club was not very busy Tuesday evening. At the moment, no one else occupied the row his locker was on, and he could overhear uninterrupted the conversation from the other side of the wooden lockers.

"That's so true. When you're young, all you want is firm tits and a pretty face. Now, it's how they use what they've got that matters. Aura is everything."

"Lord, she's got that. She is a tiger, takes charge all the way. That woman knows what she wants. And how to give it back, too."

Carter paused with one leg still out of his pants to listen, feeling a bit guilty but more curious.

"She's that way with her clothes on."

"True, but once she gets them off, there's no stopping her until she's had it all."

"I've heard she drinks like a fish."

"Like a whale. Get a couple into her, and she's ready to do it anywhere. One day after lunch, we did it in the back of the chapel."

"Downstairs?"

"Right there next to the gift shop."

"Man, Stan, that takes balls."

"Her idea."

Carter vaguely recognized one of the voices but couldn't put a face to it. The other, the louder voice of the lover, did not sound familiar.

"How did it end?"

"That's the strange part. I don't know what I did, but Friday she stops by and tells me it's over. Just like that. Finito. When she gets that way, you don't argue, you just let it go. So, I guess this one's history."

"Is that why you skipped out Saturday night?"

"You got it."

"What'd you tell Peg?"

"Said I wasn't in the mood, offered to take her to a quiet dinner instead. She jumped at it."

"Peg ever suspect anything?"

"Of me with a nun? Come on."

•••

"Whitney told me," Nathalie said. "She listened in on one of his phone calls."

"He called her from home?"

"She called him."

"When did you find out?"

"She told me Monday, but I knew before that."

"How? By the way she looked at him?"

"By the way she said his name."

"You knew but you didn't say anything?"

"I couldn't be sure. For me, I knew. But I didn't have evidence."

Nathalie hadn't been asleep when Carter called. She had just crawled into bed. Carter lay in bed himself with the television on absentmindedly, the sound off, Arsenio Hall interviewing some rap singer Carter didn't recognize.

"Why didn't you tell me?"

"Would you have believed me?"

He wanted to say that he would have, but she was right. "Will anyone else believe this?"

"You mean Fletcher? She's screwing him, too."

"How do you know?"

"Trust me."

He did. "If the convent found out, it would be the end of her—they'd ship her to a cloister in Iowa."

"Might be good for her. But it would be our word against hers. Who would the Mother Superior believe? And do you want to be the one detailing her indiscretions?"

"Seems to me I've been asked that before."

"Did either of them recognize you?"

"The guy who sat at my table Saturday night might have, but I doubt it. He hardly noticed me then. Palmer doesn't know me."

"You could tell her you know."

"Blackmail her?"

"Twelfth Step. Out of concern. I'll go with you."

"I tried that with my mother. You know how that went."

"It could be different."

"I don't think Sister X's ready for that."

"Who knows? Stranger things have happened. This may be her occasion of grace. You never know where an alcoholic's bottom lies."

"Now we do."

"What?"

"Never mind."

"Oh, I get it. Bad, Carter."

He thought seriously about Nathalie's idea. He was willing to give it a try, for Sister Xavier's sake. Besides, he had nothing to lose anyway. "Let's do that."

"Tomorrow morning?"

"First thing."

"That way she can fire us both at the same time."

Carter laughed. "I'm gone anyway, but doesn't that worry you?"

"I don't like it, but I'll take what comes. I trust if I'm not meant to be there, something better awaits me. Besides, I agree with you, the kids come first."

"Speaking of them, what about Whitney?"

"I've already set it up as part of her discharge plan to meet with Doctor Baumgardner."

Carter knew her as a psychologist who specialized in working with sexually abused girls.

"I've told her Whitney's story," Nathalie continued. "After group today, I think Whitney will go along with it. I'll make sure Doctor B. can get in touch with her if I'm no longer there."

They continued to talk late into the night about trivial things that seemed of great interest to them both at the time: her favorite pig-out food was Ben & Jerry's Chunky Monkey; he planned to buy a new pair of skatelaces before his next game. They talked well past the hour the TV station had signed off the air and the screen blurred into a blizzard of static. After they finally said good night, Carter slept soundly, the most peaceful rest he'd had in nights.

CHAPTER 22

Wednesday morning, Carter parked in the back lot. Walking in, he looked up to the row of Six West windows and what awaited him: his office, the group room, the row of boys' bedroom windows, the reception area, and Sister X's office on the corner. He had seen interventions go either way. That morning, he arrived prepared for the worst. He figured it would be a short day. He would miss the kids, especially Oscar, but he was already on his way—*he can get there without me*, Carter thought.

Riding the elevator up to the sixth floor, a calm strength radiated through Carter. Just like with the kids, all Nathalie and he could do was point out how Sister X's drinking was destroying her life. It was up to her to take action, to decide whether she was ready to do something about it. All he knew was that he could no longer keep quiet knowing what he knew and believing what he believed. For her sake. And his.

Nathalie. Carter smiled to himself. She had accepted his

invitation to dinner Saturday night.

Before he had the chance to take off his jacket in his office, Sister X buzzed Carter on the intercom. "Are you alone?"

"Yes."

"I need to see you."

"I'll be right down."

The vulnerable tone of her voice didn't sound like her. He decided to go alone and call Nathalie only if he needed her help.

Sister X did not look at him directly when he entered. Her headpiece perched crookedly atop her head, as though put on hastily. Strands of hair straggled out from underneath. Her navy-blue suit had a crumpled, slept-in look. "Sit down. Please."

She pulled a pack of cigarettes from her desk. Carter's face must have shown his surprise because, after she lit one, she said, "Fletcher's gone."

She inhaled. "Late last night. We had a terrible fight."

She said without exhaling, "I hit him."

"Did he hit you back?"

"He couldn't. He was out cold. I put some ice on his chin but don't remember what happened next. When I woke up, he was gone."

"You think he'll have HQ remove you from Six West?"

"He couldn't fire me. I know too much about him." She pulled hard on her cigarette. "He called me a whore."

"I would've hit him myself."

"He was right. I didn't love him. I only thought I did." She looked out the window. "I've been doing a lot of thinking since he left." She paused. "A lot of thinking."

He saw her face reflected in the glass. "This stanza from Psalm 51 has haunted me all morning—I memorized a lot of the psalms in Paris; they never left me.

> God, create in me a clean heart
> Renew within me a resolute spirit.
> Do not thrust me away from your presence
> Do not take away from me your spirit of holiness.
> Give me back the joy of your salvation.

"The sinner's psalm." She snorted but then said somberly, "I was wrong to try to forget it."

She turned back toward him and took another deep drag on her cigarette. "There are a lot of things I've been wrong about."

She snubbed out her cigarette angrily. "I hate these things. You don't know how much I hate these things."

He waited.

"Something you said about Oscar won't leave me alone. I thought I was in control, but my way's not working."

She sighed deeply, almost a moan. "I had nowhere to go. I was a young nun. Pregnant. The only place I could think to turn was the clinic. I've been turning away ever since."

She looked him in the eye for the first time that morning. Her eyes looked like bits of broken glass. "I can't go on like this."

When he started talking about A.A., she didn't interrupt. She seemed almost relieved when he told her the story of how he had been taken to detox, wound up in treatment, and finally surrendered. She agreed to come with him to the noontime meeting at Saint Phoenix.

•••

Carter stopped downstairs to visit his mom before the meeting. Ernie sat in the chair at her bedside, Roman collar on, oil in hand. He must have smelled the cognac on her breath because he was saying to her, "God's grace is available to you. All that's required of you is to accept it as a gift, surrender your will to his."

"Father," she said in a cracked but stubborn voice. "I asked for the last rites, not a sermon."

"God is merciful," he persisted. "He will grant you peace. But it does not have to be in death."

Her eyes remained closed. "Can we get on with it?"

"Your son is here to see you."

She must have misunderstood him. "My son shouldn't see me. Not like this."

Her voice sounded thin and brittle.

Ernie smiled at Carter with compassion.

"Will you give me the bottle?" Ernie asked. "And accept sobriety as a gift?"

"Get out!" Her face clenched in pain.

Ernie silently traced the sign of the cross on her forehead with his weathered thumb. On his way out, he patted Carter's shoulder.

Carter sat beside her on the bed. Her pale body was withered, a fragment of her former self. A thin white line of spittle coated her lips. He placed his hand gently on her arm. She jerked.

"Mom, it's me."

She opened her eyes with effort. "You're not going to preach to me, are you?"

Her breath smelled like death. He shook his head.

"Promise?"

"I'm not here to preach to you."

"Good." The spittle foamed at the corners of her mouth. "Goddamn priest."

His mind traveled back to the first time she scratched his back. He was five. In her bed. He loved it better than candy.

"A priest has the hands of God," she says.

They had stopped at Mass after a day at the arboretum. He had asked about the man on stage.

She takes his face in her hands and asks suddenly, "Do you love me?"

"Of course, Mommy."

"Promise me you'll be a priest."

"I will, Mommy."

"Promise me."

"I promise."

"Good, Carter." She scratches his back.

"Those goddamn priests—what do they know? He's not lying in this bed. He's never raised a family. He's never been married."

She coughed harshly. The spittle bubbled.

"Mom, don't you think—"

"Comes in here telling me what he knows." She wheezed. "Fucking imposter."

Carter took a deep breath and smiled at her. "Mom, I'm going to a meeting."

He bent over and gently kissed her cheek. "You're in God's hands."

He rose from her bed and walked lightly out of the room.

ABOUT THE AUTHOR

Coincidentally—much like Carter Kirchner—John Rosengren went through treatment when he was seventeen years old. He also worked as a counselor in adolescent substance abuse treatment centers. But, though he plays hockey, he never had any scholarship offers. He has written eight other books, including *Blades of Glory: The True Story of a Young Team Bred to Win* and *Hank Greenberg: The Hero of Heroes*. His articles have appeared in the *Atlantic*, the *New Yorker*, *Reader's Digest*, *Sports Illustrated*, and the *Washington Post Magazine*, among other publications. His work has won a bunch of awards, and he has been nominated for a Pulitzer Prize (but he didn't win that one). He lives in Minneapolis with his wife Maria, their two children, and a golden retriever named Maya.

See more at www.johnrosengren.net.

Mango Publishing, established in 2014, publishes an eclectic list of books by diverse authors—both new and established voices—on topics ranging from business, personal growth, women's empowerment, LGBTQ studies, health, and spirituality to history, popular culture, time management, decluttering, lifestyle, mental wellness, aging, and sustainable living. We were named 2019's #1 fastest growing independent publisher by *Publishers Weekly*. Our success is driven by our main goal, which is to publish high quality books that will entertain readers as well as make a positive difference in their lives.

Our readers are our most important resource; we value your input, suggestions, and ideas. We'd love to hear from you—after all, we are publishing books for you!

Please stay in touch and follow us at:

Facebook: Mango Publishing
Twitter: @MangoPublishing
Instagram: @MangoPublishing
LinkedIn: Mango Publishing
Pinterest: Mango Publishing

Sign up for our newsletter at www.mangopublishinggroup.com and receive a free book!

Join us on Mango's journey to reinvent publishing, one book at a time.